PRAISE FO
BESTSELLER *THE PROPHECY*:

"Gwen and Greylen are truly the power couple from the 15th century. Best book I have read all year."

—L.A. MOORE, GOODREADS USER

"A wonderful and enchanting love story with strong likable characters."

—AMAZON REVIEWER

"The story not only contains humor, but romance, action, and unconditional love...It completely pulled me in."

—AMAZON REVIEWER

"Unique, powerful storytelling carries the reader seamlessly from century to century, character to character, longing to longing, until fate unites the lovers."

—LYN, AMAZON REVIEWER

"I love time travel romances with huge hunky highlanders and this one did not disappoint."

—AMAZON REVIEWER

"Gwen's fiery and personable character charmed me."

—KAURIE, AMAZON REVIEWER

"Excellently written and absolutely enjoyable... At least for a few days, I lived in 15th century Scotland... I highly recommend this book."

—BRUCE, AMAZON REVIEWER

"This is a fabulous read, one that I really enjoyed. I found myself laughing throughout the book."

—BARNESANDNOBLE.COM REVIEWER

"*The Prophecy* will take you away from the stresses of today, and into a completely different world."

—LUXE GETAWAYS

THE PRICE

THE PRICE

LAIRDS OF THE CREST
BOOK II

Kim Sakwa

Taggart
Press

The Price is a work of fiction. The names, characters, businesses, places, events, locales, and incidents are either products of my imagination or used in a fictitious manner. Any resemblance to actual persons, living or dead, or actual events are coincidental.

Copyright © 2021 Kim Sakwa

All rights reserved. No part of this book may be reproduced in any form or by any electronic or mechanical means, including information storage and retrieval systems, without permission in writing from the publisher, except by reviewers, who may quote brief passages in a review.

ISBN 978-1-7336172-6-0

Library of Congress Control Number: 2021908382

Published in Clarkston, Michigan.

Dear Readers,

I hope you enjoy Maggie and Callum's time travel love story in THE PRICE as much as you did Gwen and Greylen's in THE PROPHECY; I am absolutely loving writing the Lairds of the Crest series!

And, if you read one of the first editions of THE PROHECY before reading THE PRICE, you might be a little confused that the Lairds of the Crest series overall has jumped back in time by 100 additional years between the two books. Allow me to explain.

I've since shifted the time setting of the Lairds of the Crest series from the 16th century to the 15th century, and all current editions of THE PROPHECY also reflect this time change.

It's all a matter of me ignoring my instincts and then finally listening to myself—and my readers! When I first started writing THE PROPHECY, I originally set it in the early 1400s. Then in subsequent edits, I moved it ahead 100 years, mistakenly thinking life in that later time period wouldn't seem so stark. But the history wasn't working quite right. Scotland in the early 1500s would have been involved with much political and religious intrigue leading to the Protestant Reformation, not to mention key activities happening in England—namely Henry VIII's selection of Anne Boleyn as his second wife and his efforts to annul his first marriage to Catherine of Aragon.

So now Gwen and Greylen's love story is back in the 1400s, where it was always meant to be—and where we also find Maggie and Callum.

There are more Lairds of the Crest novels coming soon, and I am so glad you are with me on this journey!

With love,
Kim

To my mother, Mimi, extended family, and friends—
your support means so much to me.

To my children, Ian and Blair—don't ever let the fear of failure
stop you from even trying in the first place.

And to my sister and brother, who carry the torch
of love and support our father left behind.

Daddy, I miss you every single day.

❦CHAPTER ONE❦

PRESENT DAY

Maggie Sinclair stared into the glowing eyes of the oldest living creature she'd ever seen. Searching for any hint of danger or warning—something to assure her she was the real deal. The woman, a dead ringer for the crone who gave the princess the poisoned apple, crooked a long, gnarled finger and beckoned her closer. A chill ran the length of Maggie's spine as the room fell eerily still. A gray mist rose from the old, worn floorboards reaching table height, where it stopped and hovered around them.

It was spooky and, no doubt, otherworldly in nature. Not for the first time since she'd stepped through the woman's front door, Maggie wondered what on earth she'd gotten herself into.

There were a ton of rumors about the crone. *This* crone. Rumors about predictions she'd made that turned out to be true. And how accurate they were. Maggie had never been sure what to believe about psychics or mediums, but she'd also never been this desperate.

She'd always managed to find trusted evidence that swayed her both ways at different times in the past. Maggie was trained to consider and follow evidence. All evidence. She also trained, however, to trust her intuition. Not that she had a need, or even a desire, to look into the occult before. So it wasn't something she'd ever given that much thought. Now, well, this was different.

Earlier that day, when Celeste, her-would-be-sister-in-law, suggested they come here, she didn't bat an eye.

Maggie nodded fervently and snatched Celeste's hands, surprising even herself with her sudden faith in the crone's abilities. Of course, she wanted to make contact with Derek. She wanted more than that. She wanted him back.

Period.

Two minutes later, she was grabbing a stack of money from her safe and dragging Celeste out the door.

When they'd pulled up to an odd-looking cottage with a cobblestone walk, Maggie's stomach dropped. From the expression on Celeste's face, she'd felt it, too.

They walked hand in hand on the moss-covered walkway and up the creaky wooden steps. The door opened before they'd set foot on the porch, startling them both.

A stooped woman stood in the darkened entryway, a shroud wrapped around her head and draped over her shoulders. It covered her neck and most of her features. She gestured they come inside.

Afraid she'd lose her nerve if she looked over at Celeste, Maggie stepped forward before she was able to give a second thought to what she was doing.

Now, sitting across from her—this mystic who lived on Crabapple Lane—the irony dawned on Maggie. Crabapple. Poison fruit for the princess. Witch.

In a nanosecond, Maggie became a believer.

Her eyes darted to her right, towards Celeste, who sat in the corner. Too late to turn back now. Despite looking nervous herself, Celeste gave her a hasty nod. Translation—*I'm freaked out too, but let's do this.* It was all the encouragement Maggie needed. She leaned in, fixed her gaze on the woman with glowing eyes, and tilted her head in acquiescence.

"There's a price for what you seek, child," the crone said in a serious tone.

Maggie had already decided as long as she wasn't getting a redux of Nicole Kidman's scary, abusive boyfriend come back from the dead in *Practical Magic*, she was in. She knew it wasn't rational, but grief makes you do irrational things. Maggie knew that now.

"I don't care." Maggie said, measuring her words, narrowing her eyes in determination. She wanted the love of her life back.

The old woman's wrinkled face twitched. Maggie couldn't tell if it was excitement or contempt. Something ominous in those incandescent eyes made her shiver again and swallow hard. *Stop it. Don't be a baby.*

Worried the woman would change her mind, Maggie pulled the photograph of Derek from the front pocket of the flannel button-down she wore—one of Derek's—and flattened it on the wooden table.

The picture was one of her favorites, taken at a community baseball game. Derek looked the image of health and athleticism, complete with wind ruffled hair and a playful gleam in his dark blue eyes. Careful not to wrinkle or smudge it any more than it already was, her fingers splayed on the wood as she slid the picture forward until it lay between them. Then she pushed the stack of money closer to the old woman. Celeste hadn't been sure what the woman would charge. It's not like there was a "bring my dead boyfriend back to life" special—so Maggie brought one of the emergency stacks from her safe.

Derek was all she'd had. He'd been her rock since the first day they'd met in high school, almost ten years ago. The boy who played football hoping for a scholarship had become her everything. From the moment he'd sat across from her in the media center where she tutored, they'd had an instant connection. He'd become her protector that day. And soon after, she and Celeste became as close as sisters. Maybe closer. They'd become an instant family. Not just in the way teenagers bond. Theirs had been a bond that lasted. That stayed alive and well through college and into adulthood. Like they'd always been destined to meet and be together.

Maggie would do anything, *anything* to have him back. The last month had been the worst of her life.

The old woman narrowed her eyes and fingered the stack of money thoughtfully.

When Maggie looked back at Celeste, she saw her shudder. Like the crone's look had a physical impact on her. Celeste gave Maggie a wide-eyed, *maybe-we-should-get-out-*

of-here look. But Maggie wasn't budging. She leveled her gaze on Celeste with a determined set of her chin. Celeste nodded, first at Maggie and then to the crone.

That settled, the old lady picked up the picture of Derek, then slid it beneath the neckline of her dress, tucking it against her bosom. For an instant, Maggie felt a wave of panic and almost reached her hand out, demanding the photo back, terrified she'd never see it again. Instead, she took a deep breath, reminding herself this was the way it had to be. Then she watched as the woman hobbled on ancient legs to a sideboard, where she fumbled with a small chest.

Bringing it back to the table, she brushed off the dust with her hands and opened the lid. She began to mumble to herself as she fingered the contents. Finally, the crone's eyes darted to Maggie's before she pulled out an ancient looking leather-bound ledger of some sort. Her hands swept the cover reverently before she opened it and carefully turned the thick sheets of parchment. She stopped then, tracing a line at the top of the page before reading it aloud.

"To the greatest Highland Clan, he is born," she croaked. Her voice quiet yet powerful. Maggie listened, rapt. "From a different... no... no... not this." Then, as abruptly as the crone had started reading, she stopped, casting the book aside. Maggie was startled and confused but figured magic, if it existed at all, would be unpredictable.

She was about to ask what had happened when the old woman muttered. "A doctor, a detective, and a—"

When Maggie's mouth fell open in confused shock at what she thought was the beginning of one of those stupid "a priest, a minister, and a rabbi" jokes, the hag stopped, giving her a sharp look. At this, Maggie realized with a start, *wait*, this—*she*—was the joke. Maggie was a detective at one of the country's top law enforcement agencies. She'd busted her butt to get there, too, with partial scholarships to college and law school. All that hard work had paid off. Unless the crone was referring to Derek, he was—had been—she corrected herself. Derek had been a detective as well. But who was the doctor? Maggie's mind scrambled. Was she searching for meaning where there was none? Maggie didn't know.

Maggie leaned forward to watch as the crone began fumbling again with the contents of the chest, this time withdrawing a collection of baubles. They were large stones, or jewels of some sort, in varying shapes and colors. The woman took her time inspecting several before one seemed to stick. Her eyes widened, and she visibly bristled at the first touch of a beautiful blue stone, gasping before looking up at Maggie. Slowly, she reached for Maggie's hand. It surprised Maggie how warm it was, especially since her own hands were chilled to the bone. But this woman's hand radiated heat.

Serious heat.

"Remember, child, it was you who asked," she said. Without giving Maggie a moment to react, she turned her hand over and placed the jewel she'd retrieved from the box in Maggie's palm. The large sapphire was warm to the touch—odd for a gemstone. For a second it glowed like the old woman's eyes.

"Now, go," she said. Curling Maggie's fingers around the jewel, before standing and grabbing the stack of money. "Time will tell the rest."

"Wait!" Maggie called, clutching the stone as the woman started toward the back of the house. "What am I supposed to do with this?"

The old woman turned back to her. "Don't let it go."

❧CHAPTER TWO❧

1428 SCOTLAND

Callum O'Roarke took great pains to straighten the tartan covering his wife's casket. Once pleased with his ministrations, he laid a smaller one on top of it. A symbolic piece of armor for the woman he'd wed nigh on a year ago, and a wee bit, too, for their unborn babe.

He hadn't been able to shield them in life. The least he could do is offer them some protection now, inadequate and untimely as it may be. As he bowed his head, offering a prayer that God embrace them, a heavy hand clasped his shoulder in a brotherly embrace.

Callum turned and shared a pained look with his friend.

"It's time, Callum."

Greylen's voice was a calm in the unsteady waters, through which he now waded. Callum had been lost and uncertain these past several days. Uncertain of what to do. He was grateful to those around him who did. It wasn't that he hadn't buried loved ones. He had. His father. His mother.

'Twas only this felt different. It was different. It wasn't that he didn't *know* what to do, it was that he abhorred *what* he had to do. He *knew* it was time. He simply wasn't ready. He wasn't sure anyone could be ready.

Ever.

At least not for this.

He nodded to his friend and then to the village priest, awaiting his acquiescence as it was. The doors to the keep opened, and Callum was greeted with a roar of raucous thunder.

It was fitting; he was angry too.

His wife, thick with child, had gone to help her mother. As autumn was upon them and would fast turn to winter, he'd been off attending to some much needed trades. Had he been home when word came of Fiona's mother's plight, he would have accompanied her himself.

Alas, her horse had returned riderless that very eve. She'd been found the next morn. Callum couldn't be sure what caused her to lose her seat, but she'd not survived the fall.

Now, they carried the casket containing his wife and unborn babe in a long, slow procession to the family plot, up to the top of a rolling hill that overlooked his family's land. They'd be laid to rest next to his mother. She'd see to it that Fiona and their babe would make a smooth transition to what he hoped was the pure, pearly gates of Heaven.

Callum wasn't a religious man by any means. He didn't *not* believe. It was merely while living his life, he'd taken God and religion for granted. He believed in God, certainly. He found he only had time for Him when he'd needed faith to survive. Odd, now that he thought of it. For if a man, a warrior such as he, was not weak for searching out the Mighty in his time of need, wouldn't that same man be better for it to seek the hand of God at any time? It was worth the ponder.

Once back at the keep, people lingered when what he wanted was to be alone. Even from those he was closest to. Greylen and his wife Gwen, Gavin, Darach, Aidan, and Ronan namely. They'd all come upon his door within days of Fiona's death. The men he considered brothers, or more truly brethren as they seemed cut from the same cloth, so to speak. They'd all taken his loss hard. Gwen, too, sobbing in his arms. She and Fiona had become fast friends the few times they had been together. While Gwen's outpouring had helped relieve Callum of some anguish he'd held inside, a grief he otherwise would have kept at bay—now he wanted everyone to go.

He made eye contact with Greylen across the room, who nodded in understanding. It wasn't that there were so many people there. It was just they were, well—*there*. He couldn't well throw everyone out. He didn't want to. Most lived hours, if not days, away. He wanted some solitude, 'twas all.

With Greylen's acknowledgement, Callum turned to go upstairs and was blessfully left to himself. He went to the nursery first, standing in its center. It had once filled him with hope and joy. Now he wondered what he was supposed to do with such things. The clothing and blankets Fiona had painstakingly sewn these last few months, the novelties he'd happened upon while traveling, and of course the family heirlooms passed down from generation to generation. He did the same in his own chamber. Taking in all of Fiona's belongings. 'Twas difficult seeing her hand in every place he looked.

How did one go about living amidst such... such Godforsaken circumstances? And *why?* Callum didn't know whether he was to look upon these personal items as reminders of what he'd lost, or as things he was to take comfort from.

Mayhap, in a few weeks or perhaps next month, he would place them in one of the chambers that occupied the upper floors. Or mayhap he'd add them to one of the rooms off the wing his mother had occupied. It was still full of her things. Callum had thought perhaps in time Fiona would mend some of his mother's clothing to suit. Or mayhap it would fall to their daughter one day should they have one. Now it seemed no one would have use of his mother's treasures.

He went riding that night, traversing the only place he felt a modicum of peace. The land of Dunhill. Callum rode for miles, stopping atop a crest that overlooked the sea, where he stared at the darkened sky filled with bright stars.

Anger consumed him and in his fit of rage, he wagged his sword as if threatening God himself. Furious *he*—a good man—had been dealt such an awful blow. He yelled at God, his wrath buoyed moments later as a pack of wolves joined him and howled. Thunder cracked above his head, followed a scant second later by lightning.

The storm was close.

Eyes widening, Callum watched in a mixture of awe, horror, and even a bit of peace at the irony. Here he was raging at God that it wasn't fair. That he wanted his wife and babe back. And God's bones—He'd heard him! God had heard him and was letting him join his wife and babe.

This was his last thought as a spit of lightning hit the tip of his blade. His sword set a glow as its overpowering energy ran its length... then consumed him.

CHAPTER THREE

2 YEARS LATER

Maggie wrapped her cloak tighter, belting it at the waist. She'd straightened her meager belongings on the chest against the wall, checked her *other* belongings—the items she'd 'brought' with her that weren't for public consumption—and then made her bed.

She knelt so she could feel the sword—you know, *the sword*—the one that she'd discovered tied to her old bed frame and was now tied to this one, when she felt the presence of Sister Cateline in the doorframe.

Maggie had trouble pronouncing her name when she'd first arrived. "Kat-e-*leen*" she said to herself, even now, forcing the French pronunciation into her American accent. The Sister smiled, and Maggie felt a flood of warmth wash over her. She'd come to love Sister Cateline over her time here.

Maggie hadn't been a stranger to religious cloisters. When her mother passed away, Maggie had been taken in by their Pastor and his family. The Michaels had two young girls in elementary school, and there had been a bevy of duties to oversee between the church, their parishioners, and serving the community. A boon for Maggie, she supposed. Being thrown into such a fray at a time when she needed distraction the most. It kept her busy and focused. She'd been fourteen and luckily didn't have to change schools. Ninth grade had been rough. But she'd made it, and had kept her grades up, too.

For as far back as Maggie could remember, it had only been her and her mom—until it was just Maggie. She'd never met her father, and they never really spoke of him. He was simply out of the picture.

Maggie watched her mom kind of excel at being a single parent. Her mom worked hard, had the biggest heart, and always made the best of everything. It was one of the traits Maggie admired most in her. She'd been active in their community, too. Specifically, the community center and the church. All that community meant Maggie had never felt alone. She never missed anything.

While the Abbey was different from living in her Pastor's home and spending time around her church, the order and ritual that comes with this kind of life wasn't too far of a stretch.

Time-traveling to get here, though? Well, that was an entirely different story.

For eighteen months now, Maggie had lived in Scotland with the Sisters at Brackish Abbey.

Eighteen.

Long.

Months.

She'd considered herself lucky to have found them—still did, despite Sister Cateline's overprotectiveness—considering the circumstances she'd arrived in this era. Newly and unceremoniously deposited centuries in the past, the meager and odd belongings she'd had on her person were all that she'd had to her name.

Sister Cateline had taken one look at her—her disheveled appearance, and the sword Maggie was dragging—and had known she was in trouble. She'd overlooked the obvious. Like her twenty-first century clothing, and the phone she'd kept waving in their faces, frustrated it wasn't working—and embraced her into their small convent.

Maggie thanked God every day the Sisters had somehow known Maggie wasn't a threat to them. And, more so, she'd indisputably needed them. She'd been a real mess. When she'd sunk into silence as she processed what happened those first weeks, it was met with compassion and understanding. In fact, all the Sisters were kind and motherly.

It seemed life kept upending her. Yet each time, Maggie found herself safe and protected.

Now, however, the Sisters were sending her north to a new, permanent, home. Maggie wasn't thrilled about leaving the safety of what had become her residence, here, in this century. In fact, each time Sister Cateline brought it up, which she had done almost from the first, Maggie pleaded with her to stay.

It wasn't like they didn't have room for her, and she'd always made herself useful. Even during those first few weeks when Maggie fixated on the *how* of it all. She'd mopped while exhausting every plausible explanation of what happened to her. Had sewed, or tried to—let's be honest—while tapping into that analytical part of her brain, coming to terms with the evidence around her. She'd been beating rugs when Maggie stopped denying reality, and accepted as *fact*, she was stuck in the fifteenth century.

It was then Maggie fell in with the Sisters of the Abbey. She hadn't had any luck trying to get back to her own time. So, she stopped fighting against the idea of leaving. Now she was being made to leave. Kindly, yes, and with a new home already set up for her. But leaving just the same. Sister Cateline must have had a good reason. Even if she wasn't saying it. Perhaps some change would do her good, Maggie thought now. Maybe it was for the best.

According to Sister Cateline, she'd be well cared for and, most importantly, safe. Sister Cateline's nephew had agreed to offer her sanctuary. From what the Sister had shared with her, he was a good man of solid character. In fact, she'd told Maggie, he and his companions were true exemplars of chivalry.

Maggie couldn't imagine such a saint—especially in the year 1430—but coming from Sister Cateline, that was the highest of praise. She hoped the Sister was right.

God only knew what would happen to her next. It was a sentiment Maggie didn't take lightly anymore. Life had taken a very serious turn. Considering she'd been in the process of learning how to live life again after the loss of her boyfriend, and struggling to put one foot in front of the other, well, it was a turn she never saw coming. Even now, she marveled at what had happened.

A few months after her meeting with the old bat, as she'd come to fondly refer to her, Maggie had dropped a cufflink of Derek's on their bedroom floor. Cursing under her breath, she'd knelt to grab it from where it had rolled, when she saw a large object wrapped in cloth secured to the bottom of their bedframe.

At first, Maggie thought it might be a rifle. Which would have been strange on its own, since she and Derek had never been big on guns. Other than their standard issues from the department. Even more odd, she'd never noticed it before. Obviously, she'd never looked from the angle she perched at. But they'd deep cleaned and swiffered under there plenty of times before.

Maggie swore she'd have seen it if it had been there.

She'd been going through Derek's belongings over the past few weeks. Maggie wasn't ready to part with them yet. But the longer she lived with them, and without Derek, the deeper reality set in.

The one where she was alone and had to learn how to live without him.

She had Celeste, of course, and they were closer than ever. They spent most of their evenings together, comforting each other, still. Those first few days, it had been hard to breathe. They'd literally held each other up. It didn't get much better as the weeks passed. Sometimes it was worse. But they did find some decent moments in-between.

When Maggie swallowed hard and began sorting through Derek's belongings, Celeste was there to help. Even the most commonplace items, like a spare toothbrush, or an old grocery receipt, felt significant to Maggie. The *actual* significant things, she knew, would be even harder to handle.

Maggie had decided she'd wait a year before tackling the big stuff. So finding the cufflinks was a surprise. She couldn't remember what made her lift the lid of her jewelry box in the first place, she hardly ever went in it. But it drew her eye that day and she'd stood there fingering the contents. Her mom's watch, a few pairs of earrings, and Derek's cufflinks.

Her eyes teared as she cradled them in her hand. Nostalgia overwhelmed her as she remembered dancing with him at a friend's wedding. The heat of his neck beneath her hand, the comfort of his chest as she lay her head on it, the smell of his skin. Those tangible memories were the best and also the worst.

Shaking it off, Maggie decided she'd keep them on her nightstand, just for one night. That way, when she got into bed later, she could look at them. She would reimagine the entire evening they'd been together and then cry herself to sleep. As if on cue, she tripped.

Over nothing—she looked.

One of the cufflinks dropped from her hand and rolled under the bed. It was almost comical, the slow-motion look of horror she felt cross her face, like instead of her wood floor there was an abyss beneath the bed and she'd never find it. Yet, there she was, kneeling on the ground. *That's* when she saw the large object fastened to her bedframe. Still, in the fog of grief, logic did not prevail.

Had she been in her right mind, and not panicked about the cufflink, she might have taken the time to figure out how to get to it without dragging the mattress and box spring off its foundation. But there seemed no other way.

After heaving them to the side, she'd stood there, winded, feet between the slats and still unable to feel what the covered object might be. A few other odds and ends had made themselves at home under their bed. Maggie scooped up her bag of jax, a game that had brought her comfort ever since her mother died, and shoved it into her pocket.

She wrangled with the wrapped object next. First attempting to wrench it free by brute force. Something else she would not have done had she been thinking clearly. Impatient with fiddling with the bedframe, Maggie used Derek's pocketknife to slice the thick zip ties holding it up. It fell with a thud to the floor, and she dragged it up between the slats until it lay in her lap.

Puzzled at its weight—too heavy to be a rifle—she began unwrapping it, rolling it out like a carpet or yoga mat, until she was staring at what looked like an ancient sword. Stunned, Maggie lifted it up to look more closely. It was long and polished to a glorious shine. An intricately braided pattern wound around the handle, and the hilt was emblazoned with the crest of a wolf.

The wolf is what caused her heart to pound.

Wolves had always been Derek's obsession. He'd loved them since he was a kid. He'd been so excited to discover when researching a family tree project in school, his last name—Lowell—even *meant* "young wolf" and had taken it as a sign. So that there was a wolf on this sword connected this intrinsically to Derek. At least, as far as Maggie was concerned.

Where had it come from? How long had it been under the bed? It had to be a recent acquisition. It was odd Derek had never shared this with her. Maggie didn't think he'd confiscated it from any of their cases. Derek wouldn't forgo protocol. She couldn't think of any case involving ancient swords. She wondered whether it was a family heirloom.

But still—why the secrecy?

Puzzled all the more, Maggie noticed a hollow beneath the crest that didn't seem to fit with the rest of the hilt's design. The hollow looked wrong. As if something was meant to be placed into it and was missing. Running her finger into it, Maggie pictured a jewel or carving filling the space.

Wait. Maggie's eyes narrowed as she examined the unadorned fitting, its shape and size. Something had flashed through her mind.

No, it couldn't be. She told herself her hunch was crazy. But she couldn't shake the curiosity that came over her. Keeping one eye on the sword, as if it would disappear if she looked away, Maggie went over to the dresser where she'd placed the jewel the hag had given her so many months ago.

She'd been keeping it in her pocket as instructed, and she'd gotten so used to it she barely thought about it anymore. The old bat had told her not to let it go. So, she had it with her always, except when she showered.

Maggie picked up the bright blue jewel and turned it over in her hand. She was about to return to the sword when she paused, her eyes catching one of the wolf figurines Derek used to make. He'd made hundreds over the years. Whittling them out of wood. Getting better over time, until he excelled at it. She'd been wearing a medallion she'd found in his nightstand drawer. Maggie thought at first he had made it, but it didn't have that fresh polished look of his other carvings. Still something about it compelled her, and she'd felt settled once she'd tied it behind her neck.

She lifted it now, pulling the leather cord it hung on out from under her shirt, and examined it. Maggie gasped. The wolf on her medallion matched the one on the sword. Was it some kind of crazy coincidence? Had Derek acquired it with the sword?

Phone cradled between her shoulder and ear, Maggie called Celeste, and dragged the sword back onto her lap. She pulled out the medallion again, comparing it to the crest on the sword.

They *were* identical. *Strange,* she thought.

She asked Celeste if she'd ever known Derek to have a sword, deciding it must be an old family heirloom he'd just never mentioned. But Celeste was as confused as Maggie. Heart racing, Maggie studied the shape of the hollow on the sword's hilt and turned the large sapphire over in her hand, wondering if it might fit. She believed it would. Celeste's voice sounded in her ear, insistent she knew nothing about a sword, and Maggie fit the stone into place.

Suddenly, she was overcome by a sensation much like being underwater. Maggie could barely make out Celeste's voice. It sounded so far away and distorted. Her vision blurred for long seconds before crystalizing. The jewel—the only thing in sharp focus—glowed, and Maggie heard a wolf's howl before the ground fell from beneath her and everything went black.

When she opened her eyes, Maggie found herself in a meadow beneath a tree. Completely disoriented, she did the first thing that made sense—call Celeste back.

She didn't know how long she sat there tapping Celeste's number in her address book, growing more and more frustrated when nothing happened. After accepting there was no service whatsoever, Maggie started to take in her surroundings. Looking for clues as to where she was and what had happened, her eyes landed on what looked like an Abbey of some sort in the middle of an unfamiliar field.

"There's a price for what you seek." And Maggie had just gone along with it.

It seemed fate had had something in store for her.

She still had no idea what.

☙CHAPTER FOUR☙

None too happy, his perpetual state of late. Callum held up a hand to stop Albert from going any further. All Albert said was, "The lass." Callum was tired of hearing the same concerns over and over.

With a sigh of resignation, Callum repeated himself. Again. "I've already told my aunt she is welcome here." He'd told her repeatedly the lass would have sanctuary and protection. Once in person *and* many times by letter of correspondence. He tired of saying so.

He wasn't a man who went back on his word.

Ever.

How many times did she have to ask?

His aunt had first approached him last spring, some months after Fiona had died. Given Cateline rarely left the Abbey, he'd been shocked to find her upon his doorstep. He'd told his aunt he would consider her request to house the Abbey's latest newcomer, who had no interest in becoming a novice. But that he didn't foresee taking up residence at Dunhill again until the following autumn. They'd argued then, and looking back, Callum was ashamed now that he'd lashed out.

He was angry at the time. Angry he'd lost his wife and bitter his family was gone. Seeing his aunt was a reminder of all he'd lost, including her.

Cateline left shortly after his mother died. His aunt and mother had been close. So close, the thought of being among her things was too much for her. He understood now why she'd left. 'Twas hard to live with the constant reminders.

He'd returned to Dunhill two months past and sent word to his aunt. Both in apology, and to accept her request. She'd replied posthaste, informing him they'd be underway within the week, and to send an escort.

So now what?

He looked at Albert, who had the decency to wait patiently for Callum to realize he had no idea what Albert was about to get at. Not ceding anything, he merely prompted his man. "Well?"

"Which chamber would you like her placed in?"

Callum bristled. Surely Nessa or Rose had decided such. With a small bit of irritation, he considered it now. "Put her in the chamber next to my Aunt's."

That decided, he left. His heavy footfall the only sound in the empty keep. 'Twas something he'd gotten used to.

The solitude and quiet.

Loss was a part of life. He knew this. Yet it seemed lately, loss was the only part of life he received. He'd expected it some, but had looked forward to having more in between. Love, companionship, fatherhood, a bit of merriment.

The toll of his repeated losses weighed heavily now. It showed as he looked out over the courtyard. Dunhill was not the lively stronghold it had once been. No shining beacon on the hill here. Sadly, Dunhill Proper in its entirety was running on a feeble crew, less than a score, rather than the robust staff it used to employ.

Callum oversaw much—or, in actuality, all. At least, since he'd returned. While he wasn't feeding a hundred or more, there *were* still mouths, and livestock, and crops, and the keep to oversee.

He bent now, choosing two stones, and made his way to the stables. 'Twas the one place he was comfortable.

Among the horses, the air felt different; the silence wasn't so deafening. Edward, the stable master, was mucking a stall alongside his boy. Callum smiled at the sight of them, father and son.

Maybe there was continuum after all.

Callum's horse nudged his side as he reached for the saddle. "I know, boy." He said with a firm stroke. The beast knew what he needed, and pawed the ground in a *let's get on with this* gesture. Callum was happy to oblige.

Callum and his steed made their way to the yonder hill where he took great pains to brush the dirt collected on the markers overnight. He started as always with the grave of Fiona and the babe. Then moved to his mother and father. He hadn't much to say of late. Callum spent little time anymore trying to come up with something. 'Twas merely the ritual of it that brought comfort. The rest, the reality, it just was.

After a brisk ride, he found himself ascending the stairs. If Dunhill was to be open once more, these rooms again occupied, Callum wanted to have a moment alone inside them first. He'd avoided these chambers since he'd returned to the keep.

Rooms filled with reminders of what he'd lost. In fact, 'twas sorting through Fiona's possessions months after she'd passed that had caused him to take leave. He'd finished the task, placing the items she'd treasured most in a wooden trunk he'd spent an entire month crafting. Callum had put great care into finding the perfect wood, sanding it, staining it, forging the hardware. Then he'd filled it, taking most of an afternoon to fold and stack just so—to remove and refold and stack countless times—everything, before laying on top the few items she'd sewn for the babe.

He'd knelt there long minutes, rubbing the lid with his hands. Wishing once more to feel the warmth of her skin. With a final wrench of yearning, he'd bent to touch his forehead upon the lid, then packed a bag, intent to leave before supper.

He would accept his lot in life, but that did not mean he need stay within the confines of Dunhill and its constant reminders. That was the afternoon his aunt had shown up unexpectedly, nigh over a year ago.

Now, standing in the doorway of one of the five chambers that lay between the two turrets, Callum placed his hand upon the door, his forehead above it. He was overcome with memories. Of Fiona, yes, but of his parents, too.

His father had spent years building this castle, a castle indeed fit for a queen. The love of his life, his fair Isabeau. Callum's mother had been the embodiment of love, warmth, generosity, and there was nothing his father would not do for her. Building her a castle was but one.

During his father's reign, Dunhill thrived. Scores of people worked the land, lived scattered upon it, and within the keep's walls. Shoring up Dunhill Proper and all its inhabitants was his father's gift to Isabeau and Cateline's family. 'Twas a time of growth and rebirth. Especially after the plague had ravaged the continent.

Callum did not spend long peering into the rooms. Ones he remembered as bright and filled with life and warmth. *But,* he was able to at least look within them now and think of the fond memories first. No longer was he overcome by the rawness of new grief. That was something.

As he closed the door of his parents' room, he was struck by the depth of what they shared. He'd never considered it. Not as a grown man, at least. Thinking about it now, he realized some part of him always thought he'd have it, too. He'd thought his life was in order. His path fixed and secure.

Now, considering what was and what would never be, all his mother's talk of fate and destiny seemed a fool's errand. His life had taken a different turn. Fortune ceased to provide for his family's lot.

Blessfully, his mother had not to bear witness such a travesty.

❧CHAPTER FIVE❧

Dunhill Proper, as Sister Cateline referred to it, came into view by mid-afternoon. Seeing it gave Maggie a sudden and surprising sense of relief, relief so strong it overwhelmed her. Where this feeling emanated from, Maggie had no idea. But what she did know is it consumed her so fully, her attachment to Dunhill felt soul deep.

Up until now, the thought of being separated from Sister Cateline—her lifeline in the fifteenth century—had terrified her. But if her new home included these grounds, Maggie thought she might be okay.

The property stretched for miles, beautiful rolling hills, craggy mountains, and lush waterways. She wondered, come spring, how vibrant it might look. Maggie realized what she was feeling was *optimism*, something she'd lost over the last two years.

Sure, life at the Abbey had been okay. And the nuns had been kind, but it hadn't been home. She'd spent the last year-and-a-half trying to find her way back to her own century. Or terrified the rug would be pulled out from under her again, and she'd end up somewhere even stranger.

Maggie had railed against whatever random twist in the space-time continuum had thrown her back hundreds of years, but perhaps it wasn't so random.

Perhaps fate *had* brought her here. It was possible. She was living in the fifteenth century after all.

She'd had a lot of time on her hands to consider things over the last year and a half. Like, how on earth had she ended up here in the first place? What was the whole point of *this*—her life and being here? She couldn't stop thinking about what the old bat had said. About the doctor, the detective, and how she'd cut herself off before finishing the list.

And then, of course, there had been the ominous warning. *There's a price for what you seek.*

Maggie shivered every time she thought about it. Was *this* the price? Would Maggie do her time here and then magically go home and everything about Derek's death would be a bad dream? Derek would be alive? Or they'd been mistaken when they'd taken his body away and he really hadn't died? Would she ever be able to return home? And if she did, what would she return to?

She couldn't stop thinking of Celeste, either. Maggie missed her and felt guilty she'd left her. Not that she'd done it on purpose, of course. Maggie knew what it was like to lose the people you loved and treasured. Now Celeste had gone through it twice. Once for Derek, and once for Maggie.

She and Celeste talked every day for ten years. Then poof, it was all gone. Maggie felt like she'd abandoned her. She wondered what Celeste, her coworkers, and even the

Michaels thought. Mostly, she hoped everyone was okay. That no one was worrying for her.

Maybe, by some trick of time-travel, they didn't even know she was gone. In some movies she'd seen, it worked like that.

Three hours after they'd crossed onto the land, the keep— *castle*, she corrected herself—came into view. The last thing Maggie expected to see was a... a magical castle reminiscent of a French Chateau. She looked over her shoulder, wondering if it was the sun making it appear that way.

Maggie sat up straighter, pulling her mind away from her useless questions about the how and why of it, and what's next. It was important, she make a good first impression. Wasn't it? To be at the mercy of others was the most difficult part of... well, everything.

Sister Cateline clearly had a deep fondness for her nephew, given how highly she spoke of him. While she hoped the Sister was correct in regard to her nephew's character, Maggie had seen the best and worst of people.

In both centuries now.

Honestly, it left her less than optimistic. However, the Sister had also shared with her that her nephew had lost his wife and unborn child two years ago—right around the time Maggie had lost Derek. She wondered if that might help spark some understanding between them.

As they passed through the outer wall, she was struck at the absence of people. From what she'd heard, Lairds and their lands were occupied by those under their protection. Yet, they'd seen nary a soul. Maggie laughed to herself. Since when did she say things like 'nary'?

When in Rome, she figured. Fifteenth century Scotland must be rubbing off on her.

Before she knew it, the men who'd provided escort were helping Maggie and Sister Cateline down. They kindly waited a moment before letting go. Her legs wobbled, but she recovered quickly. Maggie adjusted her cloak, then placed her hands deeper in the fur muff, hoping to look placid.

It was a look she'd tried to perfect and had plenty of practice during her stay with the Sisters.

She inhaled a deep breath as the doors to the keep opened. An older man emerged, surprising Maggie. She'd never once considered Sister Cateline's nephew would be in his fifties. But then, as the older man stood aside, another followed. Maggie released the breath she still held. Of course, Sister's Cateline's nephew wouldn't be older than the nun herself! Her relief was so great, she almost curtsied when thinking, *thank you, God.*

Appearing as serene as possible, Maggie looked up at the man coming to greet them. He was dressed in a shirt, breeches, and boots. She'd always thought highlanders wore kilts, but that craze obviously hadn't caught on yet. He was tall, broad shouldered, and moved with ease and precision. He spoke briefly to the men who'd accompanied them, before turning to her and Sister Cateline. He greeted his aunt with a kiss on her cheek, then looked to Maggie. She kept her eyes downcast so as not to appear too forthright and smiled demurely.

"Callum, this is Margaret Sinclair, your new charge."

Maggie never, ever, thought she would be someone's charge. Yet here she—and it—were.

She looked up, finally, and met his gaze. Her first reaction a relief. He appeared to be in his late twenties, or early thirties. So far, he'd aged nicely, even for the times, *like the fifteenth century,* such as these. A scar ran from his left temple to his hairline. It did nothing to detract from his looks.

In fact, it added to his appeal.

This man had severe good looks. She was surprised he wasn't already married again. Realizing she'd been staring, Maggie felt heat creep to her cheeks. Somehow, though, she knew deep down it didn't matter.

His eyes, were a deep shade of blue, filled with nothing but warmth. He felt familiar to her. Odd as it may be, she *knew* him without knowing him—she could only describe it as such.

Maggie's mind was strumming a million miles a minute, so much so, her head was literally buzzing. Leaving the safety of Sister Cateline and the Abbey was terrifying.

She felt like a little girl again being shuttled to the Michaels. They'd been a lovely family. But it had been so new and scary. Here, the Abbey was all she'd known. It had become familiar and safe. Still, Maggie knew she had to trust her intuition. She knew on some level it was going to be okay.

He spoke then. "Are you the Sister my aunt first described? Or simply Miss Sinclair?" His voice was deep, yet his brogue and Scots Gaelic easy to understand.

She'd had well over a year of language immersion to learn a few new dialects. Thankfully, there was no anger in his question or hidden reprimand, and Maggie answered him honestly. At least in this, she would start out on the right foot.

"I'm not a nun, Laird O'Roarke, but took refuge with the Sisters of Brackish Abbey. Your aunt's been very kind to me. I've grown more than fond of her, and will miss her greatly." A wave of sadness rushed over her and tears filled her eyes. Laird O'Roarke's features softened.

"You may call me, Callum," he said. "I can assure you, my aunt is always welcome. It won't be long before you'll see her again."

His compassion was almost her undoing. She bowed her head in acquiescence, which allowed her to get ahold of herself. "Thank you, for your kindness. And I, sir, prefer Maggie."

"Very well, then. Albert and I will fetch your belongings," he said, gesturing to the older man. He seemed to be a butler or valet of some sort.

Maggie only had one small trunk of belongings. A few meager items of clothing, her treasured personal items, and the sword.

That sword.

The one she'd tried to remove the jewel from every day, hoping it would take her back home. To her time. Not this century where life was stark and sometimes dank, dirty, and cruel.

She supposed she'd had it easier residing at the secluded Abbey where they lived simply, and their surroundings were sparse. The Abbey was clean, and the nuns were kind. But Maggie craved a certain freedom that had been missing.

She hoped she would fare better here, but braced herself to what she might find inside. If it were decrepit or dirty, cleaning this castle would take a lifetime. *Hey, at least that would give me something to do while I try to figure out how to go home.* So far, the jewel in her sword wouldn't budge.

She'd tried, ad nauseam.

Albert reached for her trunk, but Callum handed him Sister Cateline's satchel instead. She was again struck by his thoughtfulness. This was a good sign. Please God.

Callum carried Maggie's trunk up the steps and laid it by the door. Then went back to the cart to retrieve her sword. Maggie hoped it looked like no more than a rush or rolled up rug. He hoisted it over his shoulder and made for the front steps again.

Maggie and Sister Cateline followed. Maggie's eyes kept darting around, trying to get a lay of the land. Another internal sigh of relief upon entering. Rush covered floors, and rich fabrics ladened with filigree were placed strategically on the walls. Callum's home looked clean.

Dear Lord, it was better than that even. From what she could see, Callum's home was lovely, even for the time period.

She stumbled as her knees went weak, but Callum reached out and steadied her. Their eyes locked as his large hand wrapped around her arm. Heat consumed her from the touch, and she knew he felt it too. His eyes widened before he schooled his expression. Then, he gestured to the covered sword still foisted upon his shoulder.

"What's this?" He said, laying it upon the floor.

Maggie tried to stop him as he began unrolling it. "Wait!" She cried.

"'Tis warm. It warmed when I touched you."

At this Maggie stilled. *What on earth?* She looked to see if the sun shone in from a window, or a slit in the stone, perhaps. But of course, it hadn't. She'd been standing right there. Staring at him when it happened.

"Are you sure?" She asked. Not concerned anymore with him seeing the sword, but wondering instead what caused what Callum felt.

With a subtle double take, Callum repeated the question back. "Am I *sure*?"

Oops. Don't question the laird. He looked irritated, a look that suited him. She muttered an apology. *Note to self, Callum need not be questioned.*

"It's a sword. A family heirloom." She told him. The cat was out of the bag. Might as well jump ahead of it.

So there in the entrance of his keep, they knelt upon the rush covered floor. When he came to the last roll of burlap and it fell uncovered, his eyes shot to hers. A chill ran down her spine.

"Where did you get this?" He demanded. His voice angry and suspicious.

"What do you mean? It's mine," she said in desperation.

"This sword has been in my family for years before it was lost, nigh on two years ago."

"This sword was my—"

"Be careful!" He barked, and she drew her hand back. She'd tried to grab the blade, since his hand was on the hilt.

"Callum," Sister Cateline interjected then, "Sister Margaret—"

"She's not a Sister! And this is not her sword!"

Yikes, he was mad.

Maggie reached for the hilt then, desperate to take it back, no matter how much larger than her and stronger Callum was. In the scramble, one of her hands covered his. The other covered the stone. She would swear it was glowing now, which it hadn't done in eighteen months. She'd watched it.

Often.

Waiting for the stone to come to life again. It never had. Not since it had unceremoniously dropped her in Scotland five hundred and forty-two days ago.

Maggie froze. Was this it? Was this why Sister Cateline had been so insistent Maggie come here? Sister Cateline was very closed lipped about everything. The day Maggie had stumbled to the Abbey, banging on the doors, it was not Maggie herself, but the presence of the sword that had caused Sister Cateline to take Maggie inside.

Maggie was sure of it now. Of course, Maggie had been in distress at the time, and the Sisters were helping, but Sister Cateline's eyes nearly left her skull when she'd seen the weapon. And not in a scary *you're here to kill us look.*

Had she known bringing Maggie and the sword here would make the stone come to life again?

Was the stone going to send her back?

Was Callum coming with her?

It took her a moment to realize while the stone appeared to be glowing, that was all that was happening.

There was no blurred vision, Callum's albeit stern but handsome face was clear as a bell in front of her. The room wasn't spinning around her, and her hearing was fine. No underwater sensation at all.

She hoped the stone appeared iridescent to him, or that he noticed nothing strange at all. The last thing she needed was to be declared a witch.

Stupid hag. She hated her and pictured the crone crumbling into a dust heap, much like one of the wicked witches.

"Where did you get this jewel?" Callum asked, his voice gentler now, as he continued to finger the stone.

Maggie considered how to answer him. What was she supposed to say, the old bat gave it to me? There was a spell that time traveled her here when she placed the stone in the sword?

Yeah, right.

Instead, she went with, "What do you mean? It's part of the sword." It wasn't a lie. A stretch of the truth—sure.

He shook his head. "Nae. The jewel wasn't there." Callum didn't look up at her, keeping his gaze on the sword.

Watching him with one palm beneath the blade, giving it an appreciative once-over while tracing the handle and hilt, Maggie shivered. "Well, it would seem then, this isn't your sword," she said, trying to shake an odd feeling of déjà vu.

He smiled at her, and she almost fainted from the boyish gleam in his eye. It was a gleam of pure joy. One she hadn't seen on anyone since... well, since Derek. He'd looked like that in the picture she'd given the old bat.

The one she'd never gotten back. "Aye, Maggie, it is," he said.

It took her a moment to shake off her stupor. "How can you be sure?" She asked. He switched hands, holding the hilt with his left and held out his right, palm up.

She gasped.

Without thinking, she reached out to grasp his hand, the intricate braided pattern branded into his skin, matched that of the sword. When her thumbs brushed over the scar, her stomach lurched.

This was the third time now.

It was not a coincidence.

When she looked up at him again, she found his eyes boring into hers. It mimicked the swirling feeling she had in her stomach.

Sister Cateline interjected then, causing Maggie to jump. "Let's sort this out later. It's been a long day," she said, giving them an appraising look.

Callum tore his eyes away from her and looked at his aunt. "You know this is my sword, Auntie. You were there the day my father gave it to me."

Maggie held her breath, waiting for what she might say. This sword was all she had of value. It was Derek's. It was one of her only links to home.

Sister Cateline shrugged and said, "What am I to say, Callum. I'm old."

Maggie wondered again if she had known all along. And if so, why hadn't she said anything? She looked up at Callum then. "Please, I beg you, don't take this from me. It's all I have."

He seemed taken aback at her plea and looked down where her hands still held his. Embarrassed to find herself clutching it against her breast now, she loosened her grip. Callum removed his hand slowly, and Maggie found herself feeling the loss of it deeply.

After a long, silent moment, one in which their eyes remained locked, he stood, helping her up with that large hand of his around her arm. He said nothing about the sword, but there was a look of resignation in his eyes that made Maggie weak with relief.

She wasn't quite sure what the understanding was yet. But the thought of moving on from this exhaustive introduction and display was greatly welcomed. Without another word, Callum turned and made for the stairs. Maggie paused uncertainly, but with a nudge from Sister Cateline, she followed him, the nun and Albert taking up the rear.

Concentrating on her surroundings allowed her to calm and let the panic subside from the intensity of the sword encounter. In her twenty-first century life, Maggie had been obsessed with virtual online tours of homes for sale. She and Celeste would send links back and forth, coming up with the fictional lives they'd live in each one. The homes they chose were usually grand and elegant, but none so much as a beautiful fifteenth century Chateau Maggie had found for sale somewhere in France. Of course, that one had been restored, but this castle reminded her of that.

The stone floors and walls were light gray and scrubbed clean. Deep windowsills, framed with shutters, displayed thick cut glass. Large wood-stained beams buttressed the ceiling on the second floor. The stairs rounded the wall on the right, in a long, not too steep, ascension to the wide landing that stretched between two turrets.

It appeared there were five rooms on this floor. Each with a large wooden door set deep within a stone archway. The second room they passed was where Sister Cateline would be staying. When Albert held the door open for the nun to pass, Maggie almost gasped out loud. She'd only seen a glimpse, but her room looked lovely. Sister Cateline bid her adieu as Albert followed with her satchel. Maggie held her breath, wondering which was hers and what lay within.

Still wordless, Callum pushed the next door closest to Maggie on the right open and waited for her to enter. Stepping forward, she almost stumbled and fell as a flood of tears rushed to her eyes again. The good kind.

This was *not* the dark, dank, dirty castle one might expect of the times. Beautiful rugs covered the floors, fine tapestries hung on the walls, and rich upholstery covered much of the furnishings. *How on earth had she been so lucky to end up here? Wait... lucky?* Where did *that* come from.

The room itself was quite large, with a four-poster bed set against the far wall. A dressing area to its left, a secretary and area for personal correspondence, or what not, to its right. Lastly, an inviting sitting area arranged before the large fireplace.

Maggie spun around to face Callum, her mouth hanging open in awe. Just then, a girl entered the room and curtsied.

"Maggie, this is Nessa. She'll see to whatever it is you may need," Callum said as Nessa went right about starting a fire. Callum made a point of placing the sword across the two iron hooks jutting out from the wall, as if made and placed there specifically for a weapon. "We'll leave this for now," he said before exiting the room.

Moments later, he was back with her trunk. Setting it down, he pointed past the screen in her dressing area to another door. "You'll find an antechamber, and a personal latrine beyond." He left her then.

As Nessa scuttled about, Maggie stood in the center of the chamber. *Her* chamber. It was overwhelming, this feeling that swept through her. She'd gone from living in humble, rather stark conditions to this. Maggie was grateful for the many blessings that seemed to befall her. Not that being thrown back in time was a blessing. But with finding Sister Cateline, and now coming to Dunhill, she considered herself lucky.

While Nessa hung her shifts in the wardrobe, Maggie took her two linen-rapped bundles and discretely tucked away her treasures from home. Her phone, her jax, and the wolf medallion, she clutched under her shirt. All that had been on her when she'd arrived here.

Nessa offered to draw Maggie a bath. At Maggie's immense gratitude, she smiled broadly and showed her to the tub in the antechamber she'd already half-filled with fresh water. Refusing Maggie's help when offered. Nessa made two trips with basins of hot water so Maggie could have a proper bath.

Maggie quickly retrieved her bar of soap from her trunk, but Nessa smiled and shook her head. She opened a small hutch against the wall and took out a tray laden with soaps and toiletries. Maggie beamed at Nessa and then broke out into a laugh.

"So, this is where Sister Cateline's supply comes from? I've always wondered."

"Aye, she and Mistress Isabeau loved soaps. Callum and his father always brought them home from their travels."

After showing her where the linens were kept and laying one over a bench, Nessa left her to her privacy.

CHAPTER SIX

Callum confronted his Aunt as soon as they entered her chamber. It was next to Margaret's—no, Maggie's, he corrected himself—room. But even with the thick stone walls he kept his voice down, lest the sound traveled. "You know that's my sword."

His aunt turned and gave him a pointed look. "Of course, I know it's your sword, Callum. It's the reason I brought her here." She reached out and swatted his chest. "I've been trying to get her here for well over a year now!"

Callum sighed and nodded. She *had* tried. Her irritation was warranted. Still... "This isn't some magical Camelot, Auntie. The keeper of the sword isn't destined for, well, anything."

"She has the stone," she said. As if it had great meaning.

It was true Maggie's possession of the sapphire was unusual—confusing, even—but Callum wasn't one for machination, even those fancifully imagined as in this case. He'd wager there were dozens of places where one could get a stone to fit.

"It doesn't mean my sword has suddenly become Excalibur or the like."

"If you say so, Callum," she said, going about unpacking her satchel, seemingly dismissing his presence.

Though, Callum thought he detected a small smile around the corner of her lips. Of course, she knew she'd piqued his curiosity.

"Auntie?" He pried.

"Oh, Callum," she sighed with a wistful smile. "Your mother and I did so love the tales of Camelot, of Tristan and Isolde, of—"

"Aye, Auntie, I remember well. 'Tis the reason we've a solarium full of poetry and story filled books." His mother and aunt loved romantic tales, 'twas how his father met his mother.

His aunt came to stand before him, taking his face in her hands. "I miss her so. I can still hear her voice, Callum."

Cateline teared up as she spoke. Truth be told, he felt a rush of tears himself. His mother was all things bright and beautiful. Animated and filled with affection, she was the light of everyone's eye. His father adored her; in fact, anyone lucky enough to cross her path adored her.

Wishing to stave off the flood of emotion this reminiscence would surely lead to, or at least get ahead of it, Callum focused on his sword and the mystery surrounding it. In truth, it was never spoken of, the hollow in the hilt of the sword. Odd, he only realized that now.

'Twas as if for the entirety of his life it had no significance.

Yet, now according to his aunt, it meant everything.

"How do you know of the stone?"

His aunt smiled then, the expression causing a few tears to slip from the corners of her eyes. She took his hand and led him to the sitting area by the fireplace, a gesture that reminded him of his mother.

"Come, Callum," his mother would say, taking his hand in hers. "Come sit with Mama." She'd want to hear everything he might have done that day, or mayhap she'd tell him a funny story. When he was still quite young, she'd pull him on her lap. Her warm cheek against his temple, her lilting voice soft in his ear.

He'd looked forward to doing the same with his own son or daughter, showering his child with warmth and love the way his mother had done to him.

As Callum grew older, their fireside chats were about love, and all of its blessings good and bad. What he wouldn't give to have her with him now.

One more story... One more smile... One more anything.

She made life more palatable, no matter the circumstance. A true ray of sunshine. Even in the bleakest of times.

Callum sat with his aunt now upon one of her favorite pieces of furniture. One of many that made its way from his mother and Aunt Cateline's ancestral home in Aquitaine to the shores of Dunhill. Packed lovingly by Callum's grandsire who wanted his daughters to have a piece of home.

As his mother recalled the story, Callum's grandsire had taken his daughters to the bastide—a market town—in Libourne. He set to meet a merchant who'd written he had in his possession, many of the books his grandsire had sought for his mother and aunt. Having done business with this merchant in the past, his grandsire seized the opportunity. 'Twas said he later regretted the meeting as the merchant's friend—Callum's father—took one look at his mother and fell madly in love.

"I miss her every single day, Callum," Cateline said now. "I'm sorry you've suffered so. Perhaps I should return to Dunhill and leave the church. Mayhap Margaret was the reason I was supposed to be there."

"Of course you're welcome back any time," Callum said. "But what do you mean, Margaret is the reason you were to be there?"

"When I saw the sword, its stone firmly placed in its hilt, I knew at once there was more to Maggie's story. Your mother removed that jewel when you were nigh but a wee bairn growing in her belly, to pay for your soul's good keeping."

"We can see how well that turned out. Not the story of epic love-lore you two doted over, mine became a tragedy. 'Tis a good thing the stone returned to us, since we were so cheated."

"First of all, Nephew," she cupped the side of his face, becoming distracted as she often did when they spoke of his mother. "I miss her every day. She was my closest companion, my confidant, and... We so loved watching you grow." She smiled. "Your father, too. I'm sorry you're alone, but let's be clear... You *suffered* a tragedy; your life is not *a* tragedy."

"Tell me about the stone," he said. Not wanting to speak further of the subject.

"Ah," said Cateline, her eyes twinkling. "Now *that* is a story. Each spring your father took us to a fair, which drew people from far and wide. Every year, amidst the merchants and the livestock, there were those who practiced in the magical arts. She was tempted by many, but Isabeau said those who truly had power needn't solicit business. There was only one she wanted to speak to. The ethereal woman with vibrant eyes, who never bothered with gaudy décor or sleight of hand. This woman, with eyes that appeared to glow, needed herself and nothing more. One year, Isabeau found her and told her she wanted to ensure her son the deepest love of all."

This didn't surprise Callum in the least. His mother had always been the type to believe in magic. She believed anything was possible when it came to true love. Whatever his mother and aunt thought they'd bargained for, however, most assuredly didn't occur. Any deep, abiding love he'd had was buried yonder upon the hill. Which reminded him, he had yet to place a stone on their marker today.

"I'll never forget that woman looking at your Mama's belly, and placing her hand upon it," Cateline said after a moment, her voice gone quiet. Whatever came over her, it did much to make him realize this was not merely some fanciful tale. Whereas he was listening before with half an ear and a fair dose of dubiety, Callum was now beginning to realize the gravity of this story. "Then, she stared into your Mama's eyes and spoke in the deadliest tone I've ever heard," she said with a shiver.

"What did she say, Auntie?"

"She said, there's a price for what you seek."

"And Mama did what?"

"That evening, she removed the stone from your father's sword. Come daybreak, we spent nigh on the entire morning chasing after the group who left in the night, on to the next location."

God's bones, when it came to love, his mother was fearless. "I suppose you found her."

His aunt nodded. "The stone Isabeau paid her with is the very one set within your sword."

"You're sure of it?"

"I would stake my life on it. I tell you this, Callum Sebastian O'Roarke, your Mama brought hope and life back to this old heart of mine."

It was much to take in, this story his aunt told, and he didn't mind when she shooed him away, tired from her journey.

After leaving her chamber, Callum turned back to Maggie's closed door. Scratching his whiskers, he pondered how she'd come about the sword. Which had indeed been missing for nigh on two years now. The stone was an even bigger mystery. Maggie was far too young to be the sorceress his mother would have visited decades ago.

He'd last seen the sword that night he'd waged his fight with the Almighty and been struck to the earth in a storm.

He'd lost that battle.

His horse blessfully unharmed, though skittish, had awaited nearby. Callum had wrapped his hand and searched for his weapon, but when it was nowhere to be seen, he'd surmised it must have fallen to the sea. Later, Callum had another sword made, but it never suited him as much as the one he'd lost.

Staring at the scar on his palm, he remembered the look on Maggie's face when she'd seen it. How she'd gasped and taken his hand in both of hers. It was such an odd sensation, to be touched so reverently. To be looked at so... so curiously.

He would swear he could still feel her touch now.

Callum didn't see her again until dinner. When she entered the dining hall, the grace with which she moved struck him. A feat, considering she moved cautiously, too, like a trapdoor might give way beneath her steps. Her eyes darted to and fro. Had his father not trained him to detect such subtilties, her underlying behavior would have gone unnoticed.

What was more intriguing, was the striking contrast between her dark hair and alabaster skin. Margaret Sinclair was quite beautiful, despite the worn, plain fabric of her garment. Living at the Abbey wouldn't afford much. At least the gown fit her well, Callum mused.

As they gathered around the table, he wondered of Maggie's apprehension. Then again, she was in a strange place with strange people. When Cateline entered, there was a noticeable relaxation in Maggie's shoulders.

"Ide is a fair cook," Callum said, hoping to ease Maggie at least in that. For if nothing else, the fare at Dunhill was well above par.

"Oh yes," his aunt said, smiling as she grasped Maggie's hand. "I've kept a few things from you, sweet. You're about to discover another."

God's bones. His heart constricted in his chest at the look Maggie gave his aunt. 'Twas clear it was more than fondness Maggie felt for her.

"If this is another, Auntie," he chided. "What came before?"

Maggie looked at him then. "I had no idea your home would be so lovely."

He smiled. "Aye, my mother and Auntie's family come from great means."

"They do?" Maggie looked stunned. "Sister Cateline, you never said."

Ide, Albert, and Nessa brought in supper then. Ide always outdid herself when his aunt was in residence. She had a soft spot in her heart for her. Truth be told, Ide always supplied commendable food, even when it was simple fare.

Tonight was no different. A savory meat stew with root vegetables and thick crusty bread appeared on the table, one of his Aunt's favorite meals. Maggie beamed as he opened the tureen. She took a small portion and ate slowly, as if savoring each bite.

Aunt Cateline kept Callum occupied, catching him up on news about distant relatives. But Callum found himself drifting in and out of focus. His eyes landing time and time again on Maggie. He was watching her now as she reached to tear a piece of bread, his aunt's voice buzzing in his ear. When he passed her some butter, which was too far out of her reach, she smiled and murmured a, "thank you." Her voice soft and pleasant.

Callum noticed she eyed the tureen several times while their conversations continued. He served himself more before pushing it her way. She looked up. "Eat." He told her. "The kitchen have their own. Besides, Ide would be insulted if you didn't finish."

For dessert they enjoyed a fruit-filled pastry Ide had learned to make while last visiting the MacGreggors at Seagrave. They had an outstanding cook in residence. Grey's wife Gwen took great liberties in their meal planning, a boon to them all. If Maggie was pleased with this simple meal, he could only imagine her pleasure at... *How odd...* He had an interest in seeing her happy.

It had been so long since he experienced such, it all but knocked him off his chair. 'Twas remarkable. Something as simple as looking after someone might bring him a bit of peace, and more so, a spark of life.

Upon thinking this, he felt a twinge of guilt. Was this not abandoning the memory of his wife and babe? He shook it off and gave his attention back to his aunt, who was telling Maggie the story of how she and Isabeau first met Callum's father, and the excitement that ensued after. How their home in Aquitaine became a hub of activity over the course of the following months until the sisters made passage to Dunhill.

To hear Auntie tell it, you'd think an army provided their escort. 'Twas the men his father trusted most who accompanied them. Callum knew from his own experience, being around them as a boy, they had a way of making you feel you were in the midst of the Knights of Camelot. Callum considered himself lucky to grow up in the shadow of fearless, intelligent, and well-trained men.

Callum was surprised at the ease in which dinner progressed. In fact, the ease in which the rest of the evening did as well. After supper they walked about the main floor of the keep, showing Maggie the rooms of import, and some he'd in truth forgotten about. Then, they took a stroll, just the two of them, through the courtyard. It was a fair night and a bit early, too. Upon returning to the keep, his aunt herded them toward the Great Room.

"Maggie, dear," she said. "Why don't you fetch your game. I think the slab before the fireplace in the great hall is smooth, so as not to catch your trinkets and ball."

Maggie looked at his aunt skeptically, then at him. True, Cateline had been livelier than usual all night, raising her glass for toast after toast and talking Callum and Maggie up. Almost as if she was playing matchmaker. While Callum was enjoying her devilry, he could understand how it might be intimidating for a newcomer. He raised a brow, for he had no idea what Cateline was about.

"My aunt is alight with notions and ideas this eve, Ms. Sinclair. Who are we to extinguish her fire?" He said, hoping, again, to put her at ease.

While she made her way upstairs, he escorted his aunt into the great hall where he poured a dram of brandy in a beaker. His aunt declined the after-dinner drink and settled in one of the large armchairs before the fireplace. He took the one next to her.

Ms. Sinclair joined them a few moments later and stood before them, looking at his aunt expectantly. Callum suppressed an amused grin, even more intrigued now to know what was about to happen.

His aunt nodded. "Go on, sweet. I love to watch you play."

Maggie dared a glance his way beneath her lashes and, much to his surprise, sat on the cold stone floor. He all but spit out the sip of brandy he'd just taken when she tucked one leg in while setting the other to the side, exposing a fair portion of fine, smooth skin almost to the knee.

He watched, tilting his head as she opened a small black bag with an odd enclosure. Then, she carefully shook the contents into a pile between the v of her thighs, quickly catching a bright colorful sphere that started to roll away while a pile of silver oddities lay before her.

"Pray tell Maggie of Sinclair," he asked, intrigued beyond measure. "What have you there?"

"They're called jacks." She said, scooping them in her hand, holding them out for display. She gave him a moment to look at them, then did another dart with her eyes to him and his aunt. He saw his aunts nod and a not a second later, she softly tossed the pieces before her.

He watched her intently for several minutes as she went through what appeared to be a sequence, quite certain he'd never seen such a game. Even more certain whatever that sphere was, it was not of this world. He was reminded of Grey's wife, Gwen, who possessed her share of oddities, too.

Just then, the sphere bounced and flew his way. He caught it as one Maggie of Sinclair gasped. He rolled it between his fingers, sure it was a wonder he didn't understand.

And too, more certain something bigger was at play here.

❧CHAPTER SEVEN❧

Maggie watched Sister Cateline leave Dunhill. Her heart growing heavier the farther away she rode. Now that Cateline was headed back to the Abbey, Maggie realized she'd be truly alone. She stayed atop the steps, watching until the carriage was a speck on the horizon, then inhaled a deep, calming breath.

When she turned, Maggie was surprised to see Callum leaning in the keep's doorway. Chewing on a sprig or twig. It was a warm morning this late in autumn, and he'd loosened the ties of his shirt. The tunic reminded her of a three-quarter V-neck Henley, her favorite style to buy for Derek, only with laces instead of buttons.

For such a serious and intense man, he had an underlying quality of devil-may-care. It dawned on her then, this is what happens when the harsh realities of life catch up to you. Once optimistic and full of joie de vivre, and now painfully aware of life's arbitrary nature and the blows of reality. Left with an occasional glimpse of who you used to be, it's easy to throw caution to the wind. Be a little bit reckless. Been there, got it.

"She'll be back. Sooner than you think."

It was a kind remark, reminding her again of his thoughtfulness. Sister Cateline was right about her nephew's character. Over the past couple of days, Callum had been nothing but polite and genuinely kind. Offering to escort his aunt about the castle; always standing when she or the Sister entered a room. Maggie had even seen him take Nessa's young toddler, in a fit from teething, and soothe the little one. The latter had surprised her most.

Maggie, who'd always considered herself a good judge of character, had high hopes. Who knows, they might even enjoy a friendship. Wouldn't that be nice? To have a friend again.

"I hope so," she said, missing Sister Cateline already, the one constant Maggie had.

With a nod, Callum started down the stairs. Feeling a bit lost, and with nothing else to do, Maggie followed. He bent unexpectedly—*right there in the middle of the steps*—and she knocked into him. Lightning quick, he turned, steadying them both before they tumbled.

"Are you alright?" He asked, intently studying her face.

Maggie didn't answer for a moment, too stunned by his grip on her bicep. She couldn't remember the last time she'd experienced human touch.

Like *this* kind of human touch—held in the circle of someone's arms.

It had been years.

Heat rushed to her checks. He had her up close. Close enough, she could feel almost every inch of his impressive sinewy build. Close enough to detect a hint of pine from his recently scrubbed and shaven face. Close enough to see the bright flecks in his deep blue eyes. Close enough to feel his warm, fresh breath. Mint, she realized. He'd been chewing on a sprig of mint.

It felt like a full-frontal assault of Callum O'Roarke. She laughed, hoping to cover the odd unnamable sensation she was sure was apparent on her face.

"I'm sorry," she managed. "I was following you." Then she shrugged, still fully in his embrace and added, "Much like a puppy."

Callum chuckled, his features softening. "You'll find your way, Maggie of Sinclair."

He'd called her that last night, too, when they'd retired to the Great Hall after supper. Sister Cateline suggested to Maggie that the area before the fireplace would be perfect for her to play jax. Which brought her a nostalgic comfort as an adult. So, while Callum and Sister Cateline sat in the two large armchairs facing the fire she'd provided the night's entertainment. If you could call it that. Had paint been invented, she could charge a fortune to watch it dry. When Callum asked about it, her jax, he'd phrased it in a mysterious—"Pray tell, Maggie of Sinclair, what have you there?"—way. Made all the more intriguing as he sipped brandy from a glass beaker while the firelight played upon his features.

Coming back to his statement now, she asked, "How do you know?" He seemed so sure. As sure as when he'd caught her superball and rubbed it between his thumb and fingers before handing it back to her. Like an answer to something dawned on him.

"We all do eventually, Maggie. No matter what life throws at us."

Coming out of her musings, she asked. "You're sure?"

He considered her question, still holding her close. Any normal person would have let her go by now. Then again, Maggie wasn't pulling back, either.

Callum nodded in answer. "Aye, I'm sure of it."

"Where did you get that mint?"

He grinned, eliciting yet another physical reaction as her stomach lurched and her grip on his shirt tightened out of reflex. The soft material giving way between her fingers. Not for the first time, Maggie wondered at her body's response to Callum's closeness. Her heart and mind wanted to resist him—both for her own sake and for Derek's memory—but it was unmistakable. They had chemistry.

Real physical chemistry.

Terrified by the idea of letting herself actually care about, let alone love someone again. When she knew the absolute wreckage of heartbreak. Maggie was thrilled when Callum set her back on her feet. Finally.

"Now there's a worthy errand," he said with an annoying twinkle in his eye. "Ide keeps it in a crock on the counter."

It took Maggie a moment to remember what he was responding to. Happy to leave her former thoughts aside, she concentrated on this instead. Mint.

Buoyed with new purpose, Maggie smiled back and curtsied—jeez, there she goes again. Murmuring thanks, she made way for the kitchen, repeating "ee-da" in her head, hoping the correct pronunciation of Ide's name would finally stick.

Dunhill might be a large holding, but from what Maggie had seen there were only fourteen people in residence. Yes, she'd counted. There wasn't much to keep her sharp these days. Life moved so slowly here. So, she poured her energy into her surroundings and the lay of this unknown land.

As she re-entered the keep and passed through the vestibule, she was struck by a wave of contentment. It surprised her to realize it felt like coming home. She brushed her fingers against the fresh flowers Nessa or Rose placed in the vase. It was set in the middle of the finely crafted, and very large, stained round table hugging the curve of the stairs.

Maggie mused at how beautiful this place she would now call home really was. It was odd, this feeling. One she hadn't experienced in a very long time. It was welcome, too. Even with the confusion of, whatever it was she was experiencing with Callum.

The kitchens were in the back of the castle. Maggie had a glimpse of them, the first night here. Callum and Sister Cateline gave her a tour of the main floor. All the rooms of importance on this floor had enormous arched entryways. Some with double doors, like Callum's study, and two small parlors.

The closer she got to the kitchens, and the further back in the castle she went, Maggie noticed the inner architecture changed. Rooms here were marked with a single, albeit nicely crafted door. This was where the staff apartments were located, as well as the more utilitarian rooms. Like the sewing room, and one filled with nothing but boot polish and rags.

After a left turn at the end of the hallway, Maggie laid eyes on the kitchen. Inside, Ide and two girls were busy scuttling about. Maggie curtsied upon entering. Now a habit, she realized.

"You needn't curtsy me, sweet." Ide told her again. Her endearment reminding Maggie of Sister Cateline.

"Callum tells me you have mint?"

"Aye, and parsley. Lady Gwendolyn says their benefits are many."

Maggie wondered who this Lady Gwendolyn was. Her name mentioned twice now. After dessert the night before Callum explained many of Ide's recipes came from Seagrave and its mistress. Whoever she was, Maggie was grateful she'd brought mint to Dunhill. It was one of her favorite flavors. She hadn't had it in almost two years. On a large rectangular table pressed against the wall, Ide had laid an assortment of goodies. The aforementioned herbs, a linen lined basket of crusty bread, a platter of cheese and fruit, and a pitcher of clean water. Maggie grabbed some parsley and mint, then reached for a pear, slipping it into the pocket of her shift.

Back in her chamber, Maggie lingered by the door, touching the jewel in her sword thoughtfully. No matter the time of day, light hit it just so, making it sparkle. Though she knew now, its glittering was happenstance—not an indication of it coming to life to send her home—she gave it a customary rub with each passing.

She settled before the secretary and composed another letter to Celeste, something she'd done every day since arriving at Dunhill. What a luxury to have ink and quill. And a nice place to sit and call her own.

The view from her room, smack dab in the middle of the castle, looked out over the courtyard and buildings around it. No wonder the O'Roarke family had chosen this location as their residence. You'd be able to see who was coming and going. Especially in crisis or war. Maggie shuddered at the thought.

Later, Maggie went exploring. She spent some time looking through the shelves in the solarium. How lucky for her Callum's family enjoyed literature. Considering they were in the midst of the European Renaissance, Maggie had her pick of many literary works, religious and secular.

Imagine her surprise to find Chaucer's *The Canterbury Tales*, and Dante's *Divine Comedy*. Several tales of Tristan and Isolde, Camelot, and the Holy Grail of Arthurian legend. She chose a book on the latter, written in French. At least a language she understood, with four years in high school and two in college. Reading it might be more difficult, but she'd put her mind to it. It's not like she didn't have time on her hands. Considering how many others there were, she might as well dig in.

That afternoon, from her perch—well, it was the spot she liked best—in the great room, Maggie watched Callum enter the keep. She wondered what he did during the day. What kept him away for so many hours?

He ran his fingers through his hair, a habit she'd noticed from the first. Large hands, thick strands. He started down the hallway, towards his study, but stopped and considered her a long moment before saying, "You're safe here, Maggie."

The intensity in his eyes caused her to startle. Where had that come from?

"Why do you say that?" She asked, suddenly *not* feeling safe.

He walked up to her then and slowly reached out. His hand hovering by her neck. Maggie nodded, giving him permission to touch her, trying to ignore how the heat from his hand made her feel.

Callum gently touched the nape of her neck. Maggie shivered, remembering the feel of being held in his arms that morning. She wondered if he felt it, too. This... this whatever it was between them.

"This," he said, fingering her pulse. "Tells me you're scared."

Not everyone was trained to notice such things. Yet again, she was struck by his perceptiveness. "Just because my heartbeat's erratic doesn't mean I'm scared." Case in point, *he* made her heart race. She just wasn't sure she wanted him to.

He made a point of considering her, silent for long seconds. "Perhaps. But know this, while you're here, on my land, in my home. You are safe."

Her eyes widened. *While* she was here? Sister Cateline had made it very clear this was to be her home, but was Callum suggesting it was temporary? "Excuse me?"

He sighed. "I didn't mean to imply you *wouldn't* be here. Whatever happened before, *this* is your home now, Maggie. I swear it. 'Tis permanent."

She realized maybe she hadn't lost that nagging doubt the rug would be pulled out from under her once again. Despite settling in easily here, maybe she *did* need to hear this. And somehow, she knew it needed to be from him. There was something about Callum—never mind what his nearness did to her body—that just felt safe. Assured.

Maggie remembered the first time she'd met Derek. How he'd felt safe, too. After so many changes in her life, he'd become her instant anchor. Not just in thought or theory, but at a deep intrinsic level.

Was Callum her new anchor? Even without the teenage intensity and excitement, or the first stars of love in her eyes, Callum felt almost fated. It was a more solemn sense of fated attraction, a deeper and more soulful one, too. They were both adults, after all, and tarred from the same brush.

Callum smiled then, as if everything had been settled, and excused himself until dinner.

That evening, she met him in the small intimate dining room off the parlor, where they'd eaten since she arrived. Maggie assumed they ate there because it was closer to the kitchen than the large table in the Great Hall, and besides, it was lovely. A small fireplace warmed the entire room, and drapes hung from ceiling to floor.

She'd bathed again, a true luxury, and wore the plain shift she'd traveled in. Nessa had washed it, leaving the dress faintly scented with mint and lavender. She was a bit jittery, anxious even, since this would be her first dinner without Sister Cateline.

When she entered the small room, Callum stood and held her chair. The small action dispelled her nerves a bit. He was a gentleman, kind even. His hair was damp, and she detected a hint of pine again.

"Thank you. You're very well mannered, Callum. I'm sure your Mother was very proud."

He smiled. "Aye, she was. She taught me well, her *and* Aunt Cateline."

"It shows."

"Tomorrow, Nessa and Rose will show you the sewing room. There's a trove of fabrics to choose from. You should have a proper wardrobe."

Maggie bowed her head and thanked him, feeling a rush of gratitude. Who would have thought a proper wardrobe would mean so much? But she realized it did— even a fifteenth century one. It wasn't like she'd ever had a closet full of designer clothes. With only three plain shifts to her name these days, she welcomed any additions. New *or* hand-me-downs.

Ide brought in supper; fat roasted bird of some kind she'd seasoned perfectly, served with a savory and sweet dressing. It reminded Maggie of the sausage and dried cherry stuffing she and Celeste made for their last Thanksgiving together.

"Would you tell me of your family, Maggie?"

She'd been buttering another piece of Ide's delicious, crusty bread when Callum asked the question. Her eyes darted to his. Steady, even, grounding. He knew how to ask a question and then receive an answer. Smart man. He waited.

While he did so, she thought, why not? She hadn't spoken of her family in years. Quite, literally.

"At first, it was just my mother and I." Maggie began, willing her voice not to break. "She was great. No matter what happened, she always looked at the bright side."

She teared up then, thinking about how her mom might have handled time traveling to the fifteenth century. Would her 'the-future's-so-bright-she-had-to-wear-shades' attitude overpower the terrifying shock of it all? Most likely.

"Maggie?"

She granted him a small smile. "Sorry," she whispered, and he gave her hand a gentle squeeze. Maggie shivered yet again, she felt the touch in her stomach, like there was a direct line. She was trying to ignore it, but each time it got more difficult to do. "She died when I was a teena— fourteen. I lived with our—Father Michaels and his family after that."

"Father Michael Linton, the MacGreggor's Priest?" Callum asked.

"No, no, no." She said, dispelling his enthusiasm for whoever this other Father Michael was. "I misspoke. This was *Pastor* Michaels, someone I knew when I was young. I met Derek shortly after and we were together a little over ten years."

"What happened to your husband?"

She decided not to tell him the truth. They hadn't married. Though they'd been as good as. She and Derek had always planned on it. But there were always other goals. Careers, vacations, the house. Besides, they were very happy. A content family all their own.

"He was killed two years ago." She hadn't said that out loud in a very long time.

"I'm sorry, Maggie. What was his name?"

"Derek, Derek Lowell."

Mr. Double Take caught her mistake before she did. "You weren't married?" He looked mortified on her behalf.

She laughed. "It's okay, really," she said, patting his hand. Realizing she'd touched him too easily, Maggie pulled her hand back, but he didn't seem to have even noticed.

"How old are you?"

"Twenty-seven."

"You were together nigh on ten years and he did not marry you?"

"You wouldn't understand."

"Try to explain."

How to navigate this pickle. She burst out laughing instead. The look on Callum's face said it all; he was horrified.

"How you find this humorous is truly beyond me," he said, his eyes suddenly intense. "But I will assure you this, if there is ever a suitor, your hand will be asked for and secured."

"I don't think there will be another suitor, Callum. I'm not sure I have the heart for it."

"Ah, I know how you feel. It seems like one true heartbreak is enough, no?"

She smiled, catching herself this time before she patted his hand. "Tell me about your wife."

He poured more wine. Fiddled with his food. Then

placed his elbows on the table. Clasped his hands together, looking as though he had every intention to speak. Yet a moment later shook his head.

Poor Callum, she knew that feeling.

Maggie let the silence linger. Wanting to honor the emotions he was going through in the moment. He took a sip of wine, cleared his throat and finally said, "I loved her. She was my responsibility, and she died while I was away."

Her heart turned over for him. The things that weigh on you most.

"My apologies, I've never said that out loud."

She covered his hand with her own, no longer holding back out of some kind of made-up decorum, and gave it a gentle squeeze. "I understand." She said, trying to ignore that this poor, tortured, man was made all the more beautiful to her for his suffering. "Saying it out loud helps. If you need to, you may say it again."

It was nice having a contemporary, or not so contemporary, to share this with. While everyone had always been understanding, it never really felt like they understood. Not truly. Callum understood her pain, and she, his.

They spoke for hours then. Sometimes in hushed tones, others with a chuckle or laugh. They shared years of memories in confidence with one another. All the while, Maggie was aware this was only further solidifying whatever bond was between them.

It was cathartic and lovely all at the same time.

She'd never had someone who truly understood what it felt like to lose that one person you shared everything with. From the course of their conversation, she realized Callum hadn't either.

They didn't retire to the Great Room that night. Considering they'd spent the evening heads bent together, talking as the candle wax dripped. He bid her adieu at the top of the stairs.

With a lightness she hadn't felt in some time, she went to her room. The fire blazed, and moonlight streamed in through the window as she absentmindedly brushed the stone, now an unconscious ritual.

If she were home—in her time, home—she'd turn on some music and curl up on the sofa. Or maybe crawl into bed and read a book. Instead, she changed into a chemise. She only had two. But Nessa was quick to turn around laundered clothing for her. Maggie saw to her nighttime routine, then got into bed. She made a mental note to grab some more literature from the solarium tomorrow.

Her thoughts were rather pleasant. Which was a novelty in and of itself. She drifted off to a peaceful sleep when, true to form, her fears crept in.

Was she settling in a little too comfortably, enjoying Callum's company—and even that of his staff—a little too much? The fear of losing all she had, again, became overwhelming.

After a tortured hour or so, she finally fell asleep.

❧CHAPTER EIGHT❧

Maggie's screams woke Callum with a start. That he'd fallen asleep so quickly was itself a shock. Mayhap all that talk over supper helped. The rest spoken over dessert and another glass of wine, whilst the candles burned low, helped even more.

Her door wasn't barred and upon entering her chamber, his eyes first caught on the sapphire, aglow from the bright moonlight spilling in from the window. She'd left her shutters open, and the drapes moved with the breeze.

Maggie cried out again, drawing him to her bedside where she looked so small. Almost swallowed by the linens. Her dark hair in sharp contrast to the coverings she lay within. She tossed and turned, then sharply cried out, clutching the pendant he'd noticed her wearing about her neck since she first arrived. She usually kept it hidden beneath her clothes, but whatever it was, it clearly provided comfort.

He gently prodded her shoulder with his fingertips, thinking to awaken her. It didn't work. He pressed a bit harder, using the flat of his hand this time. Her hand clamped around his wrist like a vise, and before he could react, she yanked him forward.

A second later he lay prone on the bed, pinned beneath her elbow. Maggie's eyes flung open, wild as she panted and kept his entire arm in her hold, his thumb at a precarious angle. Had he not been so surprised, Callum would have reacted with stronger defensive precision. Yet here he was, seemingly trapped.

He wasn't in danger from the lass, but he pitied the man who was a true foe.

"Why are you here?" She asked him, as recognition set in. Her eyes darted about the room. As if danger still lurked.

"You screamed."

Her eyes shot back to him and narrowed. "I don't scream."

Callum thought better of arguing at the moment and kept his gaze direct and steadfast. Her breathing was returning to normal. Soft, warm puffs fanning the air between them.

Coming to her senses, she relaxed her grip and released his thumb. Then in a move which surprised him, she set herself down on her side with a woosh, head on the pillow, facing him.

Without mentioning the reason for his being in her chamber in the first place, her screams and obvious night terror, Maggie cupped the side of his face with her slender hand.

"I'm sorry I disturbed you," she said, sounding suddenly exhausted.

Stunned by her guilelessness, the sleepy innocence of her gesture, and once again what her touch made him feel. Alive. When he'd before been happy to go through the motions. He replied, "It's no bother."

She smiled sheepishly and like a babe sensing safety and security, closed her pretty eyes, and succumbed to sleep right before him.

Callum watched her long after, wondering what had tormented her so. None too happy to admit he liked the feel of her in his arms, now that she'd found her way there and he'd wrapped her in his embrace.

As he looked about the room, his eyes fixed upon his sword. Odd, he'd not considered it much since he'd placed it there the day she'd arrived. He thought again about his aunt's story and had to admit the reappearance of his sword, family jewel affixed in its place, *was* baffling.

For a moment, Callum wondered if it were true, this story of the enchantress and jewel. He wasn't sure if he wanted it to be. But look at Grey and Gwen. A love foretold, now stronger than ever.

Could there really be *another* prophecy exerting its influence on one of their brotherhood? Or perhaps they had been drawn together as boys precisely because of this. It was all too much for Callum. Besides, he understood how Maggie felt about the prospect of finding someone new. The prospect of losing that person.

In truth, he'd not considered it, not even once since Fiona died. He'd not considered taking another lover, another wife. Until recently. He'd thought of it since Maggie arrived, though.

God's bones, he'd thought of it more than once.

He thought of what he'd said to her earlier, about her being safe whilst under his care and in his home. He amended his statement now. "From this moment forward, Margaret of Sinclair, no matter where you go, you are safe. I swear it."

Callum awoke just before dawn, shocked he'd slept so deeply through the night. At least what had been left of it. After slowly and carefully untangling himself from Maggie, he tucked the bed coverings tightly around her. She looked peaceful once more. What was wrong with taking comfort from one another?

Truly, what? It needn't be more.

He unwittingly rubbed the shining stone as he walked past and quietly padded back across the hallway to his chamber. He couldn't help but remember how good Maggie felt nestled in his arms. Callum wondered if it was Maggie, or any other would suffice. 'Twas funny how he tried to justify it and knew it for the lie it was.

'Twas Maggie indeed.

Seven times now he'd touched her or been touched *by* her.

Aye, he'd kept count.

There was no denying, like a lightning strike, each was earth shattering.

He was just better at hiding it than she.

CHAPTER NINE

Bright sunshine and a flock of geese above the castle greeted Maggie in the morning. After having such difficultly falling asleep, she'd awoke feeling refreshed and optimistic. She stretched as she sat, bringing the sheets, which were surprisingly soft, to her face, and inhaled deeply.

They smelled of pine. The scent made her think of Callum, and she smiled remembering how his thick hair had dried over the course of their dinner the night before. His face cast in candlelight. How its flickering caught the scar across his temple.

She walked to the window, looking out at the courtyard coming to life. The few in residence scuttling about. After a moment, Maggie made her bed and saw to her morning routine. Then went in search of something warm to drink.

Each day, Ide had some pleasing concoction on the sideboard in the dining room. Today's blend was a hot tea spiced with ginger and orange. She had just taken her first sip when Callum entered and filled a large cup for himself. He made a sound of appreciation as he drank.

"I agree completely," she said, watching him.

He smiled and murmured good morning.

"Did you sleep well?" She had. Maybe all the talking last night had helped her sort through some tangled memories. Or maybe it was just that she had someone to talk *to*.

He gave her a curious an almost dubious look. "I did..." He said, then paused. "You?"

"Like a baby."

He chuckled, color suffusing his cheeks. It was very attractive. "I've instructed Nessa and Rose to make the most of the morning. As soon as you break your fast, you're to meet them in the sewing room."

"I think I'll skip breakfast," Maggie said with a grin. She'd forgotten this was the day for new clothes. The prospect filled her with excitement.

He reached out lightning quick—the man's reflexes were amazing—stopping her as she turned to leave. "Ide won't be pleased." He said, casting a look over his shoulder before giving her a conspiratorial wink. Then he grabbed a linen square and placed a large slice of what looked like quiche in its center. "This will suffice."

She accepted her breakfast-on-the-go with a thanks, and a curtsy—*whatever, so she curtsied all the time now. There were worse things in life than being well-mannered!*

Three hours and countless choices later, Maggie went in search of sustenance. She couldn't see straight and needed to stretch out her legs. Who knew how tedious and intense picking out fabrics could be?

Not that she wasn't grateful. It was a small blessing she didn't have to sew them herself. Her skills weren't great— ask the Sisters. Nessa and Rose, however, seemed to be thrilled to make Maggie a new wardrobe.

Maggie offered to help with their other duties to lighten the load, but they'd said absolutely *not*. Both times Maggie had asked. Even still, they told her she'd have at least one new garment a day.

In the few days she'd been at Dunhill, the routine was a formal breakfast and supper with the 'hospitality table', Maggie dubbed Ide's bountiful daily spread of food, in-between. She wondered where Ide had gotten that modern idea, but then considered maybe it wasn't modern after all.

What did she know of the middle ages? Besides, of course, what she *knew* of the middle ages.

She cracked herself up sometimes.

Maybe some of her mom's optimism was coming out. Or maybe it was because she'd talked about her Mom last night with Callum. It was the first time she'd recalled her so fully in years. Maggie wouldn't go as far as the-future's-so-bright or anything, but she could see, even feel things had taken a positive turn.

When she entered the kitchens, Maggie called out a hello to Ide and the girls, who *also* turned down her offer to help and shooed her away to 'the table'. Ide brought another large cup of hot tea, and Maggie grabbed some bread, cheese, and fruit. It was kind of her favorite meal.

She explored the grounds around the keep that afternoon. Maggie found two lovely flower gardens lined with hedgerows and winding paths, dotted with fountains, stone tables, and benches. A new spot come spring and warmer weather.

Walking through the courtyard, she saw Callum for the first time since breakfast. He gave her a nod, and she waved back. He bent—much like yesterday when she'd unceremoniously bumped into him from behind—and picked up two stones. Curious, she followed him into the stables and stopped short.

Magnificent is the word that came to mind. The two-story structure was large and cavernous, with at least twenty stalls. Not all were occupied. But no matter how many horses were housed here, these animals were well cared for.

Maggie loved horses. She'd attended the church summer camp as a kid, and riding had been her favorite part. She always signed up for stable duty, knowing it would give her more time with the animals. Later, when she moved in with the Michaels, time permitting, she had the luxury and free rein of the barn and stable on the church property.

"Do you ride?" Callum asked, having noticed her gawping in the doorway.

"I do. I can also clean stalls and help with feeding." She looked to the hayloft and waved back at the little boy smiling down at her.

Callum chuckled. "I don't think Edward or young Benjamin would be pleased," he said of the stable master and his son. Then he took her elbow, guiding her down the center. "There are two mares, here. We put them out every day and try to ride them. If you'd like to, you may ride one or even both."

"Really?" She beamed, letting her hand glide along the beautiful stained-wood beams that framed the stalls on either side.

He looked puzzled for only a second, then repeated. "Yes, Maggie. Really. If ever you can't see the keep, you've gone too far. It still affords you plenty of freedom. Trust me, my grandsire built this keep with that in mind. You can see for nigh on a league from its placement. Understood?"

Counting her blessings, Maggie agreed quickly. At approximately three miles, a league was plenty for now. Honestly, she wasn't sure she'd want to venture any further, anyway.

Without another word, Callum saddled his horse, gave her a nod and rode off.

It wasn't until the next day Maggie realized just how much breadth he'd given her. Sure to his word, Callum's grandsire *had* built the original keep strategically. Clear for the eye to see, even with the rolling hills, for at least three miles around.

It was on this first official ride Maggie happened upon the family plot. Beautiful headstones chiseled with the names of Callum's grandsire, parents, and his beloved wife, Fiona. Her heart broke a little when she noticed the stones on top of Fiona's marker. Now she knew why he bent in the courtyard every morning on the way to the stables.

The next evening, well after supper, Graham and Andrew returned from escorting Cateline home. She watched Callum greet them from her bedroom window.

They spoke for some time, and she found herself mesmerized. Comforted even as they conversed, nodding, poking each other, and laughing a few times. She couldn't hear what they said. But she could tell from this exchange they were close and missed the camaraderie these past few days.

She missed that, too. Camaraderie. Of course, the nuns had made her feel welcome, but she was never truly a part of their group. She didn't even have a close friend here in the fifteenth century. No one like Celeste.

Envious at the exchange, Maggie hoped she might deepen this friendship, or whatever you want to call it, now blooming between her and Callum.

She thought about what she might do on the morrow. *Yes*, that's what people said, *so what*, she liked it now. When in Rome after all. She added "taking a brisk walk in the afternoon" to her meager list of activities as she crawled into bed.

It was getting colder at night, and Nessa had wrapped a large stone warmed in the fireplace and slipped it between her covers. Her sheets still had a faint smell of pine, and she brought them to her face and inhaled. It was a pleasant scent, becoming all too familiar.

She fell asleep a short time later with a smile on her face.

❦CHAPTER TEN❧

Sitting behind his desk, Callum picked up a new block of wood and started to whittle. It had been some time since he'd done such. Years in fact. But now he had the beginnings of a growing pile of oddities.

A new set of jacks for Maggie.

He smiled, thinking of the joy it might bring her. His fingers hurt from working with such intricacy, but the practice soothed him. If only he'd thought of doing so earlier. Mayhap, he wouldn't have been so restless these past years.

'Twas a hobby he learned from his father, who was a master at the craft. Over time, Callum's skills improved, able to produce fine replicas of most anything, but his favorite objects were still the ones his father whittled. He wondered then for the first time in years, what became of the medallion his father had made for him.

Callum realized with a start he couldn't recall the last time he'd seen it. Though, it had once been a prized possession. Putting his current project aside, he spent nigh on an hour looking through his desk and shelves, but it was no use.

Mind restless, Callum stayed awake late into the night. He was happy to have Andrew and Graham back, but admitted their absence afforded him more time with Maggie. He'd enjoyed it, too.

Providence, he wondered. And not for the first time. At least since the day Maggie arrived, and his aunt told him the story of the festival, his mother's bargain for the jewel, and the mysterious enchantress.

If magic were alive for Grey and Gwen, surely it could be for him too. He'd have to be a half-wit not to consider it. The question of providence, divine guidance, or what not. She had his sword after all. The sword that disappeared the night of the storm.

He supposed it *could* be mere coincidence the Sisters took Maggie in. That she had his sword, long-lost jewel re-affixed. And every time they touched... Well, they had a powerful connection. It *could* be nothing. Something in him said it was more likely to be fate.

Life seemed a bit brighter lately; had the tide finally turned?

He chuckled. Life was more than a bit brighter. He'd been in this odd space for so long he'd not realized how encumbered he'd become. Everything weighed so heavily on him. Or so it seemed. He had duties, of course. He always had duties. Even when he'd left Dunhill for so long, he'd occupied his time with the business of helping his brethren.

He'd spent nigh on a year at Seagrave after Fiona's death. Never more grateful to not think or dwell on life. Simply do. Follow orders, give orders. Though he and Grey were equals, when together, his friend took the lead. While he was happy to provide reinforcement.

Grey knew he'd needed a distraction and had kept him busy. Mostly in training new recruits. He felt the most comfortable around Greylen and Gwen. Even Lady Madelyn, Gavin, and Isabelle when they visited, were easy to be with. There was no awkward conversation.

Instead of avoiding speaking of his loss, they asked questions and said Fiona's name out loud, rather than pretending she'd never had one. He'd found most people were uncomfortable, not just with her death but, with mentioning her at all.

Not saying her name bothered more than hearing it.

Gwen had given him one of the guest's quarters on their floor. Callum would have been happy to stay with the men in the garrison given how raw his loss still felt. He surmised later, Gwen had put him nearby on purpose.

'Twas her plan to draw him into their family, and thus back into life.

Nothing like their constant, loud banter, or having one child or another tossed in your arms oft times throughout the day to distract you. Gwen's mental aptitude in hindsight was most excellent.

Seagrave and Dunhill were entirely different holdings. Grey had hundreds of people on the land and nigh on a legion of men at his demand. While Callum presently had very few under his care. He had an army at his disposal, should he have need. Though, of late, it was only a rare skirmish at or near Dunhill. Most were aware of his skills. Of those, none foolish enough to threaten him.

The few that had, he'd dispatched with the help of Andrew and Graham.

Callum looked forward to returning soon to Seagrave. The Autumn Festival was fast approaching. The last celebration on the seashore and holding until the following spring. He planned to ride there and bring back one of Grey's carts laden with goods.

'Twas his last chance to gather supplies before winter. Not only the normal staples needed for the season, but Gwen had them all spoiled now with delicacies like olives, citrus fruits, vanilla, and coffee beans. In addition to the abundance of ingredients Grey's captains collected while traveling from port to port.

He'd be bringing Maggie with him this time. The anticipation he felt at the prospect surprised him. Based on what he'd seen of Maggie's horsemanship, she seemed proficient enough for the long ride over. He'd watch more closely to be sure, perhaps take her with him on one of his evening rides.

God's bones would wonders never cease? He, Callum Sebastian O'Roarke, was entertaining taking Maggie along on his sacred nighttime ride. Perhaps his aunt was right all along. 'Twas beginning to feel like Maggie belonged here, after all.

❧CHAPTER ELEVEN❧

A week later, another day of bright sunshine greeted Maggie when she arose. With renewed purpose and enthusiasm, she took the stairs earlier than normal, wearing the new gown Nessa left hanging in her dressing area.

She and Rose must have completed it late and snuck it in after she'd fallen asleep. It was dark blue, with pretty white stitching. They'd paired it with a thick plaid wrap that matched the color. It wouldn't replace one of her utilitarian warm cloaks, but would be perfect around the keep, and much prettier. She bounded into the kitchen, knowing Ide would still be working on breakfast. Most, if not all, the staff would eat as she cooked.

"Look." She said, standing between the large prep table Ide was behind, hands kneading dough and the one where Nessa, Rose, and Albert were. "Fashion show." She spun around and finished with a curtsy.

She kind of excelled at them now.

Her audience clapped. Even Callum, standing in the door at the back of the kitchens. She felt herself blush. Had she known he was there, she never would have done her little-fashion-show-routine. It was her third time showing off a new dress, so routine fit. He must have ridden early and taken the path by the stables and forgery that wrapped around the keep from the courtyard.

"The cordwainer should've passed through by now. 'Tis late in the season." Rose said.

"Aye, she's right," Callum said, stepping into the room. He made much ado about her new dress. Taking her hand and lifting it up high. She spun, knowing 'twas—oh, whatever, she was fully into these old-timey words by now—what he wanted. She only wished he'd stop taking her hand, every time they touched she was painfully aware of their connection. As he brought it back down, Maggie noticed the color of her dress was identical to his eyes.

"She's only two pairs of shoes," Nessa said.

Maggie tore her eyes away from Callum's. "It's fine. Really."

Callum shook his head. "'Tis not fine." He gave a nod of thanks in Nessa's direction then said, "Come, I think I have a fitting solution."

Ide handed them each a large, tall cup full of the morning's fresh brew.

"This smells divine." Maggie said as spearmint wafted through the air. Taking a sip, she joined Callum's rumbling sound of appreciation. This might be her favorite yet.

Following him through the main floor, she was surprised when Callum took the stairs and headed toward the turret at the other end of the hallway. She wondered what was behind the door. She'd explored, but it didn't seem right to delve into the other rooms on this floor. Which she knew either were, or had been, occupied by family.

"Callum, who's apartment was this?" She asked, hesitating when he gestured her inside.

"Apartment?"

Oops, guess that word wasn't in existence yet. "Chamber," she said, correcting herself. Though apartment was correct; it was an enormous space and divided into at least three areas.

"'Twas my parents' and later my mother's," he said wistfully, looking about the room as though it were filled with happy memories. "Come, I've something to show you."

Maggie stood on the threshold, taking it all in. The beautiful furnishings, the drapery, floor coverings, and all the intimate touches that made a house a home.

A pile of books still lay upon a table by the window, carefully stacked and obviously still dusted. A throw neatly folded still adorned the settee and the end of the bed. When Maggie's eyes landed on a curio, set in one corner, her heart pounded in recognition.

"Wait," she said, hurrying over to examine the dozens of wooden figurines sitting atop it. "Who made these?"

Callum picked one up. "I did." He smiled, eyes looking distant. "She kept them all, even the bad ones, from when I first started." He chuckled then, like he always did.

She liked when he did that. Color suffused his cheeks, and his serious deportment softened a bit. It was very endearing.

"May I?" She asked, gesturing to a figurine.

"Of course."

Gingerly, breathlessly, she chose a small elephant from the collection. It felt like a piece of home as she held it in her hand. "You're very good," she said, her voice thick with emotion.

She started to cry, and turned away, mortified. Callum wrapped his large hands around her shoulders, embracing her from behind.

"Maggie? What is it?" He asked softly.

It felt so good to be held by him, Maggie leaned back into his chest—until she was overcome by guilt. How could she enjoy another man's touch when thinking about Derek and home? How horrible was she?

Taking a deep breath, she shook it off, wiped her eyes, and turned. The blasted man didn't step back, and she was looking smack dab into his chest.

He lifted her chin. "What's amiss?" He asked, his eyes searching hers.

With a shrug she told him. "Derek whittled too. He made a lot of these over the years."

"In truth?"

She nodded. "Aye."

He held her there for another moment. Perhaps at a loss for what to say. She broke the silence first.

"I'm okay now. Thank you."

He seemed appeased with her answer, most likely happy to move on from her outburst. "Come." He said, leading her where he'd intended to take her in the first place. Then went down a short hallway and turned to the right, walking into a closet full of his mother's clothing.

"Oh my goodness, Callum." Her hand covered her mouth. Dresses hung everywhere. Shoes and boots lined the shelves.

"I hadn't even thought of it," he said, shaking his head. "I always entertained one day Fiona or our daughter, should we have one, might delight in my mother's treasures." He sat on an upholstered bench in the center of the room. "But what use are they now, just sitting and collecting dust?"

While she couldn't see a speck of dust. Nessa and Rose surely spent considerable time making sure this room was kept up, just like the others. She was once again surprised at the ease they were able to share their pain and deepest thoughts.

There was something quietly powerful about Callum's remembering of Fiona just moments after she had been thinking of Derek.

"Maggie?" Callum stood. "What's wrong?" He clasped her chin, tilting her head back even more, looking deeply into her eyes. After a moment, he said. "You don't have to take any of her things. I thought—"

She grabbed his wrist and shook her head, melting a little at his sensitivity. "I would be honored to wear any of your mother's things."

Truly, Maggie was touched. What she wouldn't give to have something of her mothers. For Callum to share this with her, gift it to her, was astounding and very generous.

"Come, let's find some shoes. I think you might be the same size." She settled on the bench he'd vacated, watching him peruse the shelves. "Ah," he exclaimed, grabbing a pair of flat, tall leather boots. "My mother's riding boots."

They were gorgeous boots. Maggie pulled them on, wiggled her toes, and beamed at him, they fit. "I think they're perfect!"

They shared a gleeful moment of joy. Euphoric and silly at the same time. They were only a pair of boots, but the moment had deep meaning. The leather was soft, lovingly worn and broken in. The soles felt very comfortable, as she walked from one end of the closet to the other. She sat again and looked at the bottoms. Not a scratch on them.

"Callum, these are in perfect condition."

He shrugged. "The cordwainer is exceptionally talented. He replaced the soles every year. You may take whatever you'd like, Maggie."

"I don't know how to thank you."

"You needn't," he said with a gentle smile. "You may keep the figurine too."

She almost showed him her medallion then, but something stopped her. This moment, had been perfect.

She'd wait for another time.

❧CHAPTER TWELVE❧

Callum heard the light footfall of Maggie's steps. It seemed his senses had heightened ever since she'd arrived at Dunhill. He'd been so used to solitude. Now, she was livening the premises from the inside out. As well as its few inhabitants; him included.

Ide had another mouth to feed, and an appreciative one. Maggie all but gushed her joy over every meal she was served. Nessa and Rose were able to put their skills to good use and beamed daily at Maggie's praise of the garments they made her. Even Albert had a spring in his step these days, looking after "Wee Maggie" as he liked to call her.

Aye, Maggie of Sinclair had a way about her. A way that even now urged him to leave the comforts of his study to watch as she passed down the hall. He liked how she let her hand skim the stone as she went. A delicate hand, slim and slight. Willowy in nature, she was.

It had appeal.

She had appeal.

Her daily wonderment as she continued exploring the keep was a delight to witness. He had always been proud of the home he was raised in. His father had been a simple, noble man. Not noble in station. Noble in character. 'Twas his mother, who came from true nobility and wealth. Truth be told, his mother had always been happiest giving to others. He had a feeling she would like Maggie receiving some of her belongings.

Watching Maggie now, fingers running along the wall, he followed her with his eyes. She circled the stone pillar that adorned the entrance of the great hall before flitting inside. He found her there often. It had been his mother's favorite room as well. Fiona had preferred a smaller study where she spent hours sewing and such. Not that he was making comparisons. He was just taking note of her deportment.

He realized with some surprise how much he found himself enjoying someone new about. Though, if he were being honest, it wasn't merely having *someone* about he liked, it was Maggie.

He liked having *her* about.

He liked her expressive face, framed by a mop of dark wavy hair. At times it was all he could see while she read or played her game of jacks.

It seemed of late, 'twas the first thing he checked upon coming through the doors. Her body before the fire whilst she played. Or mayhap on the chair as she read. He thought again of the upcoming trip with her to Seagrave. How much he wanted Grey and Gwen to meet her.

What he really wanted was their opinion as to why Maggie, the sword, and the jewel came to Dunhill. Could it be magic was at work here? Few knew of Grey and Gwen's prophecy.

He was one.

Maggie sat on the stone floor, legs apart, playing jacks. He loved seeing her like this. So completely at ease and focused on what brought her joy. She'd taught him how to play her strange game on one of her first nights at Dunhill.

Callum watched her bounce her funny little ball and scoop up the silver pieces a few times over before she sensed his presence. When she looked up, she blushed prettily and deposited her game pieces into the small cloth pouch he'd noticed she was very protective of.

"Would you like to play chess?" He asked, leaning over the large chair he stood behind.

While he'd be content to stand here to look upon her, he had to admit, as was often the case, he wanted to partake in something *with* her.

She darted her gaze toward his a second before she pursed her lips as if in consideration of his question.

"I don't know how to play." She said, sticking her chin out a bit.

His lips turned up at the corners. "You? Maggie of Sinclair, possessor of oddities such as jacks?" He teased, feeling the provocative air betwixt them.

She crinkled her pretty nose, then rolled her eyes. "I suppose they have value."

"*You* have value. Not your trinkets."

She blushed again and looked away.

"Come," he gestured with his hand. "I'll teach you."

He escorted her into the parlor, to the table by the window. The lighting was less than adequate this late in the afternoon, so he lit a few wicks and stoked the waning fire. Feeling her gaze as he went about the room.

When he took his seat again, she admired the pieces. "My father and I made this set." He chuckled. "Well, mostly, my father. I sanded and stained the board, however." He was momentarily surprised when she picked up a knight, the only piece with an imperfection. "If you look closely—" He went over to her, and knelt beside her, daring to lean close. Heat crackled between them, even before he covered her hand, turning the piece so the light hit it just so. "You can see where I nicked it."

She fingered the imperfection and looked at him curiously before reaching out and tracing the scar across his temple. "A twin to your wounded warrior." She whispered.

He was stunned by her stare and reverent touch, which lingered there for a moment. They held each other's gaze. Callum wondered if he ran his finger atop the long delicate vein in her neck, would it beat as furiously as his heart this very moment? Clearing his throat, he pulled back, and Maggie withdrew her hand.

Needing something to cool the heat now consuming him, Callum stood and took a detour to the sideboard where he poured two drams of brandy.

"Are you ever going to sit down?" Maggie teased in an infuriatingly coy tone.

He gave her a smirk and got back to the business of chess. Taking great pains to explain the positions and values of the pieces, and the object of the game.

"The object is to win, isn't it?" She asked.

"Aye, in this game the object is to win."

Her head tilted, the light casting part of her face in shadow. He was so intrigued with her. Mayhap, enjoying this game before chess, more than she.

"Are you saying that's not always the object?" She asked.

'Twas an interesting question. Perceptive too. It made her all the more appealing. "To most the object is always winning, Maggie. In some cases, a true win means a draw or surrender."

"Winning sounds better."

He chuckled. "My friend Grey would agree." Thinking now might be a good time to bring up Seagrave he broached the subject after she finished her move. "I have need to travel in a few weeks. I would like you to come."

In serious concentration of the board, her eyes darted his way, glinting mischievously. "Are you trying to throw my game?"

God's bones this attraction was powerful. "Strategy, Maggie of Sinclair. Strategy."

"Hmph," she said, quite adorably. "Tell me *Callum* of O'Roarke, what would this 'traveling' you have need of entail?"

Enjoying her wit, he told her, "A day's ride to a lodge built by myself and my father. Followed by another quick jaunt of mayhap the morning."

"I see. So, a day and half of travel." She leaned back, steepled her fingers and gave him what he was sure was a mimicked look. "And pray tell, Callum of O'Roarke, what else?"

He chuckled, finished his dram and spelled it out. "After our travels, we would be guests for nigh on a week of my closest comrade, Greylen MacGreggor and his wife, Gwendolyn."

Her eyes went wide. "A week?"

"Aye. You have my word, you will like Seagrave and our hosts." With that he made his next move.

She took note of the board, then looked back to him. "A week?" She asked again. As if uncertain about being away for so long.

"Aye, I've need to collect supplies for the winter. Grey and I will spend a day or two sorting through inventory. Even if that were the only reason to journey, Gwen would never let me... *us*, stay only a night or two. Then, of course, there is also the lively celebration to attend."

"Ah, how clever. Waiting until the last to tell me the *real* reason," she teased. She looked a bit worried and said, "I'm not sure I have anything to wear to a celebration. I'd hate to bother Nessa with it."

"You have the correct attire already," he said, hoping to put her at ease. "I guarantee you'll be comfortable and fit right in."

She finished her dram and looked at him pointedly as she made her next move. "Okay," she said, more like herself. "I'll go."

CHAPTER THIRTEEN

"Fetch a cloak, Maggie."

Callum stood in the entrance of the great room, a fur draped over his arm. Her head shot up, startled by his gruff tone. Her shock quickly turned to glee—looking at him standing there, eyes dancing with excitement, she realized what was happening.

She stared for all but a second, then ran for the stairs. A rare and early snow dusted the Highlands, and he was taking her riding!

Although Callum had given her access to the stables and free rein with the horses, he'd never taken her on one of *his* rides. It was like being invited into a private club.

The *real* club.

She made it to her room and raced back down, breathless and more excited than she cared to admit, her new riding boots on her feet. Without another word, but clearly suppressing a grin of his own, Callum opened the door and let her pass beneath his outstretched arm before pulling it closed behind them.

She tried not to skip, but she may have, which made him laugh.

He caught up with her at the bottom of the keep's front steps and took the lead. Maggie paused a moment to take in the scene. As the full moon illuminated this beautiful man's form, he laughed again, like a carefree boy.

Grinning, Maggie trotted to catch up to this new side of Callum and followed him to the stables. When he gathered the mare she'd become terribly fond of, her nose crinkled in delight.

"Oh, I love her, Callum."

He smiled. "I believe the feeling is mutual."

When he turned in the direction of the saddles and riding gear, she stopped him. Even as a young girl, Maggie enjoyed the process of tacking up her own horse.

"I've got this," she said, already reaching for her favorite saddle.

He nodded and went for his horse, a magnificent specimen of a beast. They seemed to get along well, her mare and his stallion.

She noticed the stallion nudge Callum's pocket. Callum reached in and retrieved a few carrots, handing her one for the mare.

As they prepped their horses, Maggie and Callum fell into a companionable silence, as was becoming their habit. Finally, Callum reached for the fur he'd brought and draped it around her.

"Ready?" He asked, placing a hat on her head.

Maggie could only nod. It was one of those perfect moments. The kind that strikes you like a lightning bolt in case you were about to miss it.

She'd just reached for the pommel and placed her foot in the stirrup to hoist herself up when Callum's large hands, one cupping her bottom, the other around her thigh, deposited her atop the saddle.

At first, it offended her, that he thought she needed help. But then she realized two things. One, Callum was always thoughtful. She liked that about him. And two, she also enjoyed being touched by him. Her heart was still racing when he mounted his steed beside her, and they left the stable.

A full moon lit the entire countryside, as wispy snowflakes dusted the air. It was glorious.

After an hour of an easy ride, Callum turned to her, his boyish smile lighting up his face. "Ready?" He asked again.

She grinned back and spurred forward, racing across a clear, flat stretch of meadow. She'd never seen this side of him. How suddenly unburdened he seemed. His energy was completely different.

When they approached a brook, Callum motioned for her to slow down and pull her horse to a stop. After dismounting, he brushed the snow from atop her shoulders, then laughed and put a hand on either side of her head to shake off what had accumulated on her hat.

The horses drank, and so did they. Then they were off again.

They stopped on top of a crest that overlooked the entire valley below. It was breathtaking. Callum removed a canteen of sorts from his jacket and handed it to her so she could drink first.

By the time they returned, it was very late. Her cheeks flushed from the cool night air, but she felt terribly warm inside. They stayed with the horses while they cooled down and spent another hour brushing, praising, and giving them treats.

They were quiet again as they walked back to the keep and took the stairs once inside. Maggie turned as they separated at the landing.

"Thank you, Callum."

He gave a smile and nod, reaching out to brush her cheek with his hand. "You're welcome, Maggie."

It was a lovely end to a wonderful night.

CHAPTER FOURTEEN

Awoken by what sounded like a stampede in the courtyard, Maggie grabbed her robe and hurried to the hallway. She ran into Callum, already dressed in his usual shirt, breeches, and black Hessian boots, sword in hand.

"I heard riders," she called out, slipping her arms through the sleeves of her robe as he headed for the stairs.

When he turned, she noticed something very different in his manner. Something she'd never seen in him before.

Power, authority, and a deadly seriousness.

She could feel it from twenty paces away and shivered as he strode toward her. She almost backed up. That's how intense and remarkable this change in him was.

"Go back to bed, Maggie."

There was no affection in his eyes, no momentary softening. Nothing. It was as if the man she'd left a few hours ago was gone.

In his place was this... This—warrior.

He opened her chamber door, and she went back inside, obedient. Once he closed the door behind him, Maggie ran to her window.

A group of at least ten men on horseback were waiting by the keep's doors. When Callum appeared, he greeted them, but didn't stop, making his way assuredly to the stable where Edward had already saddled his stallion and was bringing him into the courtyard. He leapt atop the steed, motioning for the men to follow.

She watched them go.

He never looked back.

She didn't go back to sleep that night. When the sun rose, she left her chamber and spent the entirety of the day pacing outside and in. Poor Ide brought her small bites to eat, but Maggie was too nervous to be hungry. She nibbled on the food to be polite, but so overcome with worry, it was the last thing on her mind.

No one knew anything about what had happened, or where Callum had gone. Only Albert seemed to have some information. When Maggie asked him, all Albert said was trouble had occurred—which could be a million things—and that Callum was needed.

When dusk approached, Albert appeared atop the keep steps and insisted she come inside. Reluctantly, Maggie obeyed, but continued her pacing and worrying in the foyer. An hour later, Albert approached her again with another affectionate but stern look and sweep of hand. She'd been banned from there as well.

It was close to midnight when Maggie took yet another turn at one end of the hearth in the great room. She froze when she saw him standing in the archway. They shared a look as relief swept through her. A bit of the Callum she knew was visible on his face. But he didn't move, so she rushed over to him, alarmed even more.

"Are you okay?" She asked, checking for herself. Like a statue, he stood there as she basically felt him all over. "Say something!" She yelled in her desperation to figure out what was wrong with him, sweeping her fingers through his hair. Then she felt it and pulled her hands back.

Warm, sticky blood covered her palms, and Maggie screamed.

She faintly remembered him trying to calm her. Ide coming in and handing her something warm to drink. Callum made sure she drank it all, then escorted her to her room, where Nessa was waiting, and helped her to bed.

The last thing she remembered was Callum at her bedside. His hand pressed to the side of her face before his fingers swept through her hair, brushing it away.

She remembered, too, feeling loved and safe.

❦CHAPTER FIFTEEN❦

'Twas some time now since Maggie called out in her sleep. Though Callum knew her lack of night terrors was a good thing, there was a part of him that enjoyed comforting her in the middle of the night. Even if she hadn't remembered his care in the morning. In truth, it did not surprise him to hear her screams tonight, considering her distress when he'd returned home earlier.

He padded down the hallway, opened Maggie's door, touched the talisman, and crawled into bed beside her. She clutched whatever she wore around her neck, but kept it hidden, as always. He'd grown more curious about what it was. But at that moment, he shushed her until she quieted and settled in his arms.

He recalled the night before last, when those blasted trespassers had called for his attention. Of all the nights for trouble to occur, his maker had to choose that one.

Which had been perfect, up until that moment.

Now, the evening ride with Maggie was marred by what followed. Apparently, God, or whomever controlled the fates, wasn't done with Callum yet.

More than that, though, Callum thought about the moment of his return. When he'd stood in the threshold of the Great Hall and saw her. 'Twas like a vise released within his chest. He had frozen at the sight of her beauty, and safety, and warmth after a night that was anything but.

The relief upon her face when she'd seen him was one brandished in his mind. How she'd rushed to him, her pale and upturned visage framed by her glossy dark hair. She'd given him a thorough once over. Gasping at the blood on the back of his head. He hadn't time to tell her his wound was of no consequence. Suffered in the face of poachers trying to divest him and a neighboring clan of their property. The problem had been dealt with handily.

She'd been inconsolable. Her look turned to horror. 'Twas no other way to describe it. Even though he was standing right in front of her, sound and whole—at the sight of his blood on her hands, it seemed—she was caught in a memory.

He'd seen such looks before. God's bones, he'd had them himself. Set off by a sight or smell and confronted squarely by a memory you wished you'd never had.

Grateful now to hold her even for but a few hours, they slept soundly. She with a wee bit of help from the curative Ide had prepared post haste.

Later that morning, she greeted him in the small dining chamber. Callum hoped she might remember his ministrations this time, but it didn't seem so. When she'd sleepily asked why he was there and he'd told her about her fright, she sighed and said once again she wouldn't have screamed.

Apparently, one Maggie of Sinclair preferred to downplay the obvious. Determined not to dwell on the feeling of her body nuzzled up against his, he pushed such thoughts aside.

He'd almost choked on a fine bite of Ide's omelet moments later, when without pleasantries or subterfuge she made a request.

Refusing to believe he'd heard correctly, Callum took a long sip of his tea to recover and looked at her.

"I asked if you would show me how to use the sword," she repeated.

That she'd said *the* sword and not *my* sword was most likely the reason he even entertained her request. "I heard you."

She rightly didn't chastise him for making her repeat herself. "Well?"

"I... I—why?" He truly couldn't imagine *why* she would want to.

"I'd like to know how to defend myself. How to defend you, even. Dunhill. Our home."

Stunned by her statements, in truth, *stunned*, he could only stare. He knew of women who were proficient with a sword, 'twas unusual but not unheard of, but that her reasoning included protecting him and "their" home, struck him soundly.

She must have sensed his silence had some significance because she left her solicitation and the reasoning behind it hanging, and went back to eating. She said nothing more on the subject.

He'd weighed her request for the rest of the morning.
He thought about the sword, too. It was odd his attachment
to it seemed changed. It bothered him not that it still hung
upon the wall in her chamber. That the jewel drew him each
time he passed it and he touched it as if in superstition.

Yet, not once since he'd placed it there, had he wanted
to take it down. To feel its weight in his hand, it's helve in
his grip.

'Twas midafternoon when he'd made his decision. He
found Maggie in the Great Hall, head buried in a book.

"Fetch your sword." He said, pensive and deadly
serious. Although he would teach her this, he was not happy
about it.

Her head shot up at once. A myriad of emotions
crossed her face. Then she ran for the stairs.

Callum was a master swordsman. Few reached the
skill set he and his brethren achieved. He'd taught young
boys to wield a weapon in the past, so he could surely teach
Maggie as well.

He knew she would be proficient. She was fit and
agile, an accomplished rider, and conditioned by her long
walks about the property. But holding, hefting, and *wielding*
a weapon of this size, this weight, and one so deadly was
nothing to trifle at.

Outside, she followed him down the front steps and
toward the courtyard. When they reached the spot upon
which he practiced, he could tell from her stance she had
been watching these past weeks.

To test her mettle and basic instinct, Callum begun
this lesson as he had countless others before, by startling

Maggie into reacting. He spun on his heels and swung his sword up toward her in a wide arc. He watched the shock and anger light her features as she realized he'd begun an offence. But there was something else in her eyes, and quite frankly, it shocked him, if not filled him with pride.

Reflex, skill, and a fighting spirit.

'Twas elementary at best, but Maggie brought her sword up to block the blow. He knew the impact was jarring, saw her wince, and guessed she was most likely nibbling on the inside of her cheek.

He was sure if he circled her arm with his hand, it would still be vibrating. Buoyed by her visceral response, he swung back the other way. He was ambidextrous when it came to swordplay. The arc coming from that side confused her, and she froze before regaining her wits. She did her best to quickly bring her sword back up, barely before impact. He knocked it from her.

Shaking her hands against the burning sensation common to the uninitiated, she bent to retrieve it. He stepped across the blade, stopping her.

"What are you doing?" She spat bitterly. "If you don't want to teach me, then don't. But don't treat me like this."

"Why is this so important to you?" He pressed.

"I already told you, Callum."

He shook his head. "Nae, 'tis more. Something happened. Last night, when—"

"I can't protect you. I couldn't protect him!"

"Who?" Callum asked. He paused, catching the look that passed over Maggie's face. Then he realized. "Derek?"

God's bones. What happened to give her this fear or need to protect him, protect them?

"Yes, Derek. They killed him. He died in my arms."

Ah, so there it was. Poor, Maggie.

His heart broke for her.

Callum reached down to help her up. She hesitated a second before she grasped it. He lifted her to her feet. Then picked up her sword and extended it to her. She looked at him, a bit leery.

"Let's start with the fundamentals."

"Much like we should have?" She said, arching her eyebrow.

He smirked. Then spent the next hour taking her through a grueling routine. The best had trained him and he did so in return. Then he ordered her to a soak in a hot bath and receive her dinner in bed.

He did not see her again that evening and imagined she was asleep before her head hit the pillow.

❧CHAPTER SIXTEEN❧

With the help of Nessa and Rose, Maggie packed for the trip to Seagrave. Callum had somehow remembered she'd only had her trunk and left two matching satchels on the bench inside her room. A note pinned to one read:

> Maggie,
>
> *As my mother is no longer traipsing the countryside, she would have loved for you to have these for your own travels.*
>
> *Callum*

She hoped that meant she could take both. It wasn't easy packing for a full week, what with the seasons changing and with her fifteenth century clothing being especially bulky. But Nessa and Rose rolled and folded her dresses with ease. They even made sure to leave her garments for the night at the lodge and the next morning on top.

Maggie was nervous about staying with people she didn't know. But Ide told her Seagrave was a lovely place, and the MacGreggors were as fine as people could be. Considering Ide could only be comparing them to Dunhill put Maggie at ease. At least a bit.

They left as the sun began its rise. Maggie dressed for the cold in a soft wool dress, a cloak Callum insisted she use, another treasure from his mother's closet, and of course her boots. Her sword was secured to her saddle, as well as the new satchels filled with a few changes of clothing. Callum had the same, plus a bow and quivers.

With a long day ahead of them, Callum estimated making it to the cabin with just enough daylight for him to secure dinner. He said they could take their time the following day since Seagrave was only a few hours ride from there.

They kept a steady pace throughout the morning, heading due south before turning westward. Ide made a hearty lunch, her crusty bread filled with some roasted fowl Maggie decided was chicken—as she did with all the mystery birds Ide cooked—herbs, cheese, and fruit tarts. Each of the three times they'd stopped so far, including lunch, Callum insisted they drink plenty of fresh water, as did their horses.

By midafternoon, Callum pointed out the last crest before their final decent. He said the lodge was built at the base of the mountain, close to a large brook.

When they arrived, Callum saw to the horses, while Maggie grabbed some wood from a stack outside. A pouch with flint and steel was on the hearth, dry tinder in the fireplace. It took a few strikes, but it wasn't long before the fire was crackling.

She opened the shutters, did a quick dusting, shook out the linens, and swept the floor. In short order, the quaint one-room cottage was clean and warm. By the time she unpacked their bedclothes, Callum was back.

"What's for dinner?" She asked with a grin.

"Salmon." He said, holding up two large bundles of freshly caught fish, he must have cleaned and wrapped by the brook.

She laughed. "You left with quivers and a bow." She said, thinking for sure he'd bring back something like a rabbit.

"I wanted to so see if the edges of the brook had started to freeze over. Our luck, dinner awaited my arrival."

"How are we supposed to eat all that?"

He grinned. "I've seen you eat," he pointed out. "And I've a hearty appetite tonight."

While the fish roasted, Callum brought in a few buckets of fresh water, placing them on the hearth to warm. They sat on the floor before the fireplace. He'd cut the fish down the center and roasted them with the skin still on. Together, they plucked the meat, still hot, but so succulent.

"Oh my God, Callum." Maggie groaned in appreciation with each bite.

He smiled, that boyish gleam in his eye, and reached out to wipe something from the side of her lip. It was an intimate gesture, one of many they shared now. God help her.

No, really, God help her.

She wasn't asking to go back home. She wasn't asking for Derek back. She wasn't even asking for the last year and a half to be different. But in this... *please*...

She felt it and knew he did, too.

She didn't want to act on it or assume where it may be going. Honestly, it terrified her and excited her at the same time. That feeling of being in love you can't tamp down. The one that gives you a rush and makes your heartbeat so fast you worry it will explode. Yeah, that's how Callum made her feel. She had to stave it off.

Toe that line in the sand and DO NOT CROSS.

By the time they finished their supper, the water had warmed to just above frigid, and they cleaned up. She was about to wash her face, but he stayed her hand. Then went to a small hutch next to the bed. He pulled out a fresh linen square and a small tin, opening it before he handed it to her. She wondered if it was Fiona's. Seemingly reading her mind, Callum shook his head. "'Twas my mother's."

It hit her then, the truth about what and how she felt. At fifteen, she wasn't capable of feeling this. Not that she hadn't loved Derek, of course she had, with her whole heart. But the feelings she had for this man were fuller, deeper, more mature. Where they each were in their lives, the things they'd experienced, she wasn't sure if she'd ever felt what she was feeling now.

She'd been so young when she met Derek. The love had been there, but it had been a different kind of love.

Guilt gnawed her heart, leaving Maggie both content and confused.

The soap smelled of flowers and citrus. Exotic ingredients indeed. "This is the good stuff," she said. He gave her a smile, waited while she washed and did the same with his pine infused soap.

❦CHAPTER SEVENTEEN❦

Callum leaned against the door frame, watching as Maggie walked along the edge of the reeds. She'd wanted to stretch her legs before they set off. Yesterday had been such a long day that truthfully, they'd eaten supper and fallen asleep quickly afterwards.

He'd laughed when she'd told him she'd sleep by the fire. He told her there was room aplenty in the bed, then gave her some privacy while he checked on the horses one last time. When he returned, Callum changed and lay on the other side. At times he felt guilty for the feelings he had for her and wondered if Maggie struggled, too.

She looked back now and waved, then grinned and pointed to the ground. Aye, must be a rabbit or two crossing her path.

He laughed when she did it again; her joy infectious, even at this distance. She followed after them, quickening her strides along the perimeter of the vegetation between the meadow and the brook. The rabbits darted through the reeds toward the water. As Maggie, caught in her innocent glee and curiosity, turned to follow them, dread swept through him as his stomach fell.

Nae... Nae, Maggie—the ice!

"Maggie!" He called. Cupping his mouth, he tried again. But he could see from the tops of the reeds she was moving further away.

He ran, his heart pounding furiously in his chest. *God's bone*s. He was halfway across the meadow when he heard her scream.

Nae! NaeNaeNae!

"*MAAAGGIE!*" He bellowed.

Running toward the sound. He took small solace the closer he got, the louder he heard her struggles, more welcome than silence. The water was freezing, she'd survive that, 'twas the vegetation beneath that was a death trap. He ran through the same path she'd taken and saw her as soon as he cleared it.

"*Maggie!*"

She looked up then with a labored gasp as she struggled to free herself. Her eyes filled with dread. He could tell she was trying to untangle her legs from the vines beneath the water. She stared at him, her big eyes filled with resignation.

Nae, He would not lose her.

He shook his head as he dove in. The water burned. He reached her in seconds, grasping her shoulders, trying to lift her higher, if even for a moment, until he freed her.

She stuttered, "I... I..."

"Shhh, I know. Be still. Promise me, Maggie, be still while I untangle you."

She nodded and he dove beneath the water.

With his dagger, he cut through the vines tangled around her legs. Pulling her away quickly, lest she get caught again. He cleared the deadly area with her in tow as he surfaced. It was easier getting in the water than out. But he managed to reach solid ground.

Then he ran with her in his arms the entire way back to the lodge as she tried to speak. He slammed the door behind them, grabbed the blankets from the bed, and set her down in front of the fireplace. Barren now, since they'd been ready to leave.

"C—c—" She stuttered.

"Shhhh." He pulled off her boots, surprised they were still on, rubbed her entire body from head to toe, dragging off her dress as he went.

"C—c—Ca—llum... s—so..."

"I know. I know. Cold," he finished for her, panting himself. Caught in the franticness of the moment while divesting the last of her underpinnings.

She was deathly pale and shaking badly. He wrapped her in the bedcoverings, all of them, rubbing her arms and legs. Then grasped her head within his hands. "You will be fine, Maggie," he said harshly. More for his ears than her own. "I need to start the fire again."

She nodded, teeth chattering now.

He almost ripped the door from the frame when he went to collect more wood. Bringing it nigh back to roaring, felt like it took precious minutes he didn't have. He stripped out of his own wet clothing and grabbed another blanket to wrap around his waist. Then he pulled Maggie across his lap, rubbing her arms and entire body. Finally, he just held her tight, rocking her back and forth. She was shaking from the inside out. He could feel it.

Then she halted.

"Maggie, look at me." He grasped her chin, seeing her lips held a blueish tinge. He needed to get her warm.

None too gently, he lay down with her on top of him and wrapped them together beneath the blanket, flesh to flesh. She was so cold to the touch, it burned against his skin.

He covered her lips with his, blowing slowly and gently to warm her. It didn't take long, before he was rewarded with a moan. A moan of life, not of passion, there was a marked difference. She mmmed as he continued his ministrations. Slow breaths, in and out, arms clutching her as closely as possible.

Long minutes later, he felt her lips warm and begin to swell within his as he continued to breathe upon them... over them...Her body relaxed into his, and for the first time since she'd turned to chase those rabbits, he breathed a sigh of relief. Reflexively, he gathered her closer.

Her eyes opened then, and he could see from her gaze that he needed to stop. He felt a moment of deep sadness as he removed his lips from hers.

Feeling at once bereft. It took every vestige of willpower to not cover her mouth once more and in truth, kiss her.

There, he thought it! God, strike him. He'd had his lips on her, and he wanted to kiss her.

Kiss her, in truth.

He wondered how she would feel if he did. He tucked her head in the crook of his neck lest he try, and gathered her close. She leaned into the embrace, sighed, and within seconds relaxed into a deep slumber.

It struck him as he held her, as much as they, or at least *he*, liked to think they could merely remain friends, he loved her.

Aye, he loved her.

She was easy to love. Kind, caring, reserved, enchanting, his charge. It was more than the love of a family member or one in your care.

She would not be pleased.

He was struggling at the moment, too. He'd never thought to feel like this again. Quite honestly, he wasn't sure if he ever felt like this. His feelings on that were mixed.

Instead of leaving early, he held her in front of the fire for hours while she slept. Twice he'd gotten up to add wood to the fire. The second time he'd put on a dry pair breeches, then joined her once more beneath the covers.

The first time he'd wrung out her dress and hung it close to the fire, to dry. That's when he saw it.

The medallion she always wore. The medallion he'd swear to his dying breath, his father carved for him nigh on fifteen years ago.

Margaret Siobhan Sinclair was wearing his medallion. It was this fact or *artifact* that sealed her fate.

Let it be so.

CHAPTER EIGHTEEN

Even from afar, Maggie could tell Seagrave was one of the most incredible places she had ever seen, and considering Dunhill, that was saying a lot. There was an enchanting quality about it, and from the first, she felt this constant buzz of activity humming through it, this underlying current of revelry.

But something had changed drastically between her and Callum, and they were still working their way through it.

It started as soon as they arrived on the MacGreggor property. Within seconds, four men on horseback surrounded them and Maggie began devising a plan to systematically take them down one at a time, wishing she'd had a few more lessons with her sword. Then she realized they were friends.

"O'Roarke." One said, followed by similar greetings.

"Who's this?" Another asked.

It took less than ten seconds of their welcoming smiles, for her to feel something in the air change between them. Not her and Callum, but Callum and these men. They were subordinates, not his equal.

Then God help her, Callum staked his claim, revealing a side of him Maggie had never seen before—changing their dynamic once and for all. No longer could Maggie rest in the self-assurance they were "just friends."

"*She* is with me," Callum said, his voice firm.

Not *she is my charge, treat her respectfully or be on your best behavior.* Or even, *Maggie's not looking for a suitor. We have some unrequited feelings and things happening between us, so give us some time to figure that out first.*

Nope, he didn't imply anything of the sort. He might as well have said, "She is mine."

She must have said it aloud, because one of the men pointed out. "He did lass, he just dressed it up so as not to disturb you." Then he gave Callum a nod, and the men scattered.

"Callum—" Maggie started, thrown off by his change in demeanor.

Who was this gruff, headstrong, possessive man? It dawned on her then, the other time she'd seen him like this. *This* Callum was the same man who'd been called upon to dispel trouble that nerve wracking night weeks ago.

A warrior.

"Don't." It was all he said.

The look on his face gave her pause from pushing the subject. They hadn't spoken of what happened at the cabin yet. In fact, she hoped they never did.

She'd sum it up with, it was a scary event and Callum saved her. Who cares that when she'd heard him yell her name, the panic and fear in his voice pierced through her heart and made her regret they would be lost to each other?

Or when he was in the water telling her to be still, she was frantically committing his face to memory, hoping to take it with her. Who cared that when they were skin to skin, his mouth on hers she felt the single most earth-shattering moment of her life?

How many of those was a person supposed to have?

She'd had her share!

She didn't want anymore.

Presently, however, she wished to give a few of them back considering how rude, insensitive, and overbearing he was acting. A warrior on the battlefield was one thing. She didn't want *this* Callum by her side always.

Was this how it was going to be?

By the time they crossed the courtyard, all the castle's inhabitants had crowded on the front steps. And they *were* impressive steps, stretching across a fair portion of the keep, but even so it was *a lot* of people.

That's when she noticed the couple standing front and center. A stunning strawberry blond and a... a... a God.

"Holy mother—"

"He's married," Callum bit out giving her a scornful look.

Wow, he *was* touchy. She feigned a wounded look. "Ouch."

He shrugged. She wasn't having any of his pity-party or whatever it was he was having.

The gorgeous woman standing next to the Adonis passed her toddler to one of the many outstretched arms and made her way towards them.

Adonis followed.

Callum slid off his horse like a seasoned Hollywood stuntman, landing with grace before embracing the woman who came to greet them. He clutched the arm of, who she assumed was, Greylen MacGreggor and did a kind of shoulder-bump-guy-thing hello.

Then Callum was at her side. Not that she needed help, but there were so many people. She had to concede it was nice having him near. Maggie knew he wasn't really trying to insult her with his dig before.

It dawned on her, he must have been jealous. She almost made a joke about it as he reached up for her with his large hands and circled her waist to lift her down. As always when he touched her, she became momentarily distracted. He gave her a pointed stare before brushing the hair off her shoulders, taking great pains to smooth the back.

He may as well have lifted his leg to mark his territory.

"What are you doing?" She ground out as quietly as she could.

He shrugged. "Helping you down," he said rather absently.

"Except you made a point to fix my hair, Callum. In front of—" Sweeping her arm, she gestured to the crowd. Her words trailed off when she realized how closely they were being watched. Gwen and Greylen were staring at them with expressions somewhere between joy and shock.

"It's not what you think." Maggie said, shaking her head.

They exchanged a look, then said at exactly the same time. "Then what is it?"

"Leave her be," Callum told them. "Grey, Gwen, this is Maggie Sinclair. Maggie, this is Laird Greylen MacGreggor and his wife Gwendolyn."

They both said their first names at the same time, in a let's-be-on-a-first-name-basis-and-cut-through-the-pleasantries sort of way. Her conversations with Callum were deep and intimate, but he wasn't the verbal sparrer Greylen and Gwen appeared to be. She could tell they were feistier, fierier opponents, both in fun and in argument.

She'd have to sharpen her skills. Immediately.

"So, what is it?" Greylen asked again.

"Oh, Husband, stop." Gwen said, latching her arm through Maggie's.

In a move that felt choreographed, Gwen started herding her towards the steps and away from the men.

"Halt." Greylen's voice was dead serious now, confirming Maggie's thoughts—it *was* a choreographed move. Gwen had known what she was doing when she'd tried pulling her away. They turned back to Greylen, who directed his next question to Callum, his tone cooled considerably. "Is there something we should know?"

Callum ignored the question and gestured to her horse, "Maggie, take your sword."

Good Lord, she was so flustered she'd left it without a thought. She grabbed it now.

"*That* is not her sword, Callum." Greylen said, he'd gone from friend to formidable in three seconds. "That's

Lyall ore, forged for your father and extolled with your family crest."

There was a load of information in that statement. Maggie repeated it in her head so she could play it back later. For now though she said, "Possession is nine tenths of the law."

At this Gwen gasped, giving Maggie a wide-eyed look that startled her. While Greylen's own eyes narrowed.

"Whose law?" He demanded.

"It's just a saying," she said with a shrug, taking a cue from Callum. Going for the draw, rather than the win.

Gwen tightened her hold on Maggie's arm and continued to look at her curiously.

"We have a saying here as well, Maggie," Greylen said drawing Maggie's attention back. "Do you want to tell her?" He asked Callum, "Or should I?"

"Stop it, all of you," Gwen said, finally finding her words.

Hurriedly, she ushered a still-confused Maggie away. The men didn't interfere this time. To be honest, Maggie was happy to get away. From all of them. Especially the crowd still on the steps hanging on their every word.

Be gone, people!

You'd think the Seagrave courtyard was a stage where dramatic events often took place or something.

They passed through the front doors, and if not for Gwen's death grip on her arm, Maggie would have stumbled into the palatial, two storied foyer. Instead, she just tripped, looking up at the grand staircase worthy of any royal.

"Gwen, I'm going to lose this limb if you don't ease up," Maggie hissed. Something was clearly afoot, so she kept her voice low to avoid drawing prying eyes or ears.

Gwen immediately loosened her hold but didn't slow her pace. Urging Maggie forward, she whispered, "Why did you say that?"

Something in Gwen's tone stopped Maggie short. "Say what?" She asked.

Gwen leaned in closer, her eyes darting around before fixing them on her. "You know." She tilted her head then, eyes bulging, trying to draw it out of her, whatever *it* was.

Truly, Maggie was at a loss. The look on Gwen's face made it hard not to look away. The nervousness in her eyes made her want to. To see who Gwen thought was watching them.

"No," Maggie whispered. "I don't know. What did I say?"

"That possession-is-nine-tenths-of-the-law." When Maggie still didn't answer, Gwen continued, "You know, an expression that doesn't *exist* yet in the frigging 1400s?"

Maggie's head reeled back. "You too?" She asked, barely able to let herself believe it.

Gwen nodded furiously, as a flood of relief washed through Maggie. *She wasn't alone, not anymore.*

Gwen must have felt it too, because right there before the staircase, they both teared up, nodded, and hugged. Overcome, Maggie tried to hold back her tears. She felt like she'd found a piece of home. Not *her* home, but home as in the twenty-first century home.

Soon, three men closed in on them, each sounding concerned and inquiring a frantic, "Lady Gwendolyn?"

Gwen sighed, wiped her eyes and waved them off, "I'm fine. Really."

"So, we *were* being watched," Maggie said.

Gwen snorted. "They're harmless," she laughed softly. "Well, to me at least. They're *way* overprotective. They'll ease up once they get used to you being around."

The men nodded like this was a good thing, and she waved them away. "We have much to discuss," Gwen whispered leaning in again. The men apparently interpreted Gwen's shooing of them as stand two feet away instead of just one. An adorable toddler wobbled towards them and Gwen bent to pick him up. "Well, it may have to wait until later, but let's get you settled."

At that, Gwen turned on her heel, beckoning Maggie to follow. For a moment, Maggie stood where she was. Still in disbelief at what she discovered. Her eyes landed on an enormous picture window that looked out at the sea.

Maggie felt a moment of peace.

A moment was all she had just then, as Gwen kept a quick pace. Maggie had to trot to catch up to her. They turned to the left and Gwen led her down a wide hallway to her room.

"This is so lovely, Gwen." Maggie said, feeling like she stepped inside a luxurious hotel suite—well, minus the mini bar and TV.

Gwen pointed to a pair of hooks on the wall where Maggie set her sword. There was a sitting area before the fireplace, already lit and roaring. A large bed flanked by side tables, and what looked like a comfortable armchair. An arched door was set into the wall to the left.

"There are a few books on the table. I'll show you our library tomorrow," Gwen said, then paused. "You're staying the week, right? Callum told you about the festival—"

Maggie smiled. "Aye, we're here for the week."

She sighed then. "Good, okay, there's a wardrobe and dressing area here. We've made all these chambers ensuites." She opened the door. "You should find anything you need in the drawers. Well, except for an electric toothbrush or hair dryer. Oh, that reminds me, I'll bring you some make-up later."

"Make-up?" Maggie asked, realizing only now how much she'd missed dressing up.

"Well, it's really just a brush and powder I use for eyeliner. And an ointment of Lady Madelyn's—she's Greylen's mother, you'll meet her tomorrow. She's been at Gavin and Isabelle's for a few weeks now. Isabelle is Greylen's little sister. And Gavin, well, Gavin is our best friend." She shrugged. "It's a long story, but we kind of share him. Gavin was Greylen's first-in-command, but when his father passed away Gavin became Laird. They just finished building their home and Lady Madelyn was helping them with the baby and the twins. Am I rambling?"

Maggie laughed. It *was* a lot of information. "Wait, Mom, sister, brother-in-law, got it." She said, noticing something didn't seem to add up. "This is so different. So much livelier than Dunhill. I know Callum is—"

"Oh, Callum is Laird of Dunhill. It's a lot to learn, I know. When I first got here, I was always mistaking Lairds,

Lords, and Barons. It's very confusing. Anyway, don't let Dunhill's present scarcity fool you. He's very powerful and Graham is his first-in-command. If Dunhill were running at full speed, it would be similar to Seagrave. Well, minus Greylen's merchant business. *And*, now I'm getting carried away again. Come," she said, taking Maggie's hand and leading her toward a very comfortable sofa. "I have so many questions, Maggie. How did you come to be here? What happened?"

Maggie shrugged, truly at a loss. "I guess I made a deal with the devil."

Gwen shook her head. "No, I assure you, you haven't. Not if you landed here... Or more to the point, with Callum. That was no deal with the devil. He's a good man, Maggie."

Maggie was stunned by Gwen's statement. How it seemed Gwen was completely content here, in the fifteenth century. As if given the option between staying here and going back home, Gwen might actually choose to live in the 1400s. Maggie realized with a jolt she might be beginning to feel the same. When was the last time she'd tried to magic herself home?

If she were being honest with herself, she *did* feel like she'd landed in a good place.

And, yes, *with Callum*.

Even now, with his whole one-syllable-word-warrior routine. Seriously, they'd spoken only a handful of words since they'd arrived at Seagrave and frankly none were great. Yet, all of that aside, deep down she'd been more than content lately. Here was someone from the twenty-first century who truly looked and sounded— "You're really happy here, Gwen?"

"Oh, Maggie," she said, reaching over to take her hand. "Yes. It sounds crazy, maybe, but yes. I love sitting in my home, watching my husband walk by speaking to his men, or holding one of our children. I love our family dinners, which are usually a large affair. You've come at an odd time, I swear, our table nearly bursts. It's simple, yet complicated in an entirely different way than back home. But you know what I love most? I'm not sure I would have found this anywhere else." She looked up a moment, then covered her heart. "This feeling of belonging somewhere and to someone. Don't let these archaic trappings fool you. Greylen and Callum are wealthy, intelligent men. They're well-schooled, and I truly believe the 'thinkers' of this time." At Maggie's wide-eyed look, she said, "I kid you not. There isn't anything they can't imagine—or won't—if it means the safety and sanctity of their loved ones, their family, or their clan."

They heard Callum call out then, and Gwen stood, toddler and all, "We'll talk more later. And remember, if you had to 'land' somewhere, you did okay. Trust me."

Stunned, and oddly more comfortable than she'd felt in a while, Maggie stayed on the sofa staring at the open doorway Gwen left through.

❧CHAPTER NINETEEN❧

Callum took the stairs warily. God's bones, in the blink of an eye, everything had changed. There was no mistaking the feeling that had consumed him when Kevin and the other men had come to greet them once they'd crossed MacGreggor property. The moment they'd cast appreciative smiles at Maggie, he'd been filled with jealousy. The gauntlet of possession fell, and he'd all but marked her for everyone to see.

Not very nicely, either.

He'd ignored Greylen's questions as James, the stable master, came to collect their horses. Callum said a few perfunctory hellos to the other familiar staff and grabbed his belongings *and* Maggie's and went inside. He called out for Gwen, who appeared atop the landing as he started up the stairs.

She gave him a tenderhearted look. "Same chamber as always."

"And Maggie?"

"The one after."

He turned atop the landing, passed his room and put Maggie's satchel down on the bench just inside the open door. She looked right at him, shocked, bewildered mayhap. Maggie may as well take her pick considering his behavior, but she said nothing. He couldn't blame her.

After a quick change of clothes, he started down the stairs, surprised to hear Maggie call after him. He turned and met her halfway.

Still at a loss for words, he remained silent, unsure what to expect. Whatever it was he may have presumed, it was not the olive branch she extended in the form of her—*his*—sword.

He was stunned by her graciousness.

Then again, they *were* tarred with the same brush, as she'd said. The stumbling blocks of one step forward and two steps back. He supposed they'd both made considerable progress. If not for Maggie, Callum wasn't sure he'd be in the place he found himself now, wavering on the edge of a new life.

What happened at the cabin had a considerable impact.

With a genuine nod of gratitude, he accepted her gesture of goodwill and exchanged swords with her. She nodded back, and along with a formal curtsy, went to her chamber. Though the entire interaction occurred in silence, it cemented the shift he had felt between them.

Eager to dispel some of his restless energy, he met Grey on the practice fields. In short order the years fell away, as was always the case. It felt like the days of yore when they'd first become brothers-in-arms.

They'd been but five and ten years of age, when Dar, Aiden, and Ronan had joined in their ranks. All five were soon sworn into a sacred brotherhood one brisk autumn evening by Grey's and Callum's fathers. 'Twas the true reason for the Autumn Festival, though most weren't aware—'twas their way to honor their fathers.

He remembered something then, that it had been his mother's idea they should all have medallions with their family crests. "Future Lairds of the Crest," she'd said.

Callum wondered for what felt like the hundredth time where Maggie had come by the one she wore. It was so like his, it could only be the same. The same medallion his father made.

But *how* could that be so?

Whatever the answer, it had no bearing on his feelings for her. 'Twas merely that seeing it, at that time, had seemed... well, fated. He looked up at the sky, a silent thought of his mother and what she may have brokered. He felt an intense pain in his head then, and would have sworn he saw stars before all went dark.

Sometime later, Callum awoke in his chamber, startled to find Maggie sitting on the bed next to him. He was in pain, too. A vague memory of Greylen's sword coming into contact with his head just as he'd looked up at the heavens.

Ah, he thought. *Never lose focus on your opponent. Even if he's your brother.*

Through the walls, Gwen was yelling at her husband. Though, that was nothing new. Callum chuckled, a sorry move considering his throbbing head. The feel of Maggie's slender hand gently stroking the unwounded side of his forehead was the most pleasant sensation he'd felt... well, since his mouth covered hers at the lodge, whilst enfolded in his embrace.

She looked down at him with her pretty eyes. Her hair fell about his face.

God's bones, he was in trouble.

Gwen bustled in and asked nigh on a score of questions. "What's your name?"

"Callum O'Roarke."

"How old are you?"

"Two and Thirty."

"What year is it?"

"1430."

She rolled her eyes. "Don't remind me." Then she leaned in close and whispered. "Do you know where Greylen keeps my Christmas gifts, and the extra brandy?"

Callum chuckled. "If I did, I'd not tell. You know we've an oath betwixt us."

"Whatever." Seemingly satisfied, she pressed a fresh cool compress to his head. "Rest until supper please. I'll check on you then."

"I'm fine, really, Gwen. Thank you."

"You gave Greylen quite a fright. There are very few people he likes sparring with. From what I understand, he was 'all in' so to speak. Your luck he has good reflexes and turned his blade. You could be missing a chunk from your head or worse."

"I'm sorry, Grey." He called to his friend who had appeared in the doorway.

Greylen shook his head, still looking shaken.

"Rest." Gwen said again. "And no swords play for two days. We'll see you at supper. It's just the four of us tonight."

Gwen and Grey left then. Leaving him alone with Maggie. She started to move, and he was surprised at the panic he felt. He stayed her with a hand. "Please. Don't go."

"I wasn't going anywhere. Can I get you anything?"

He shook his head, regretting the action and winced. Maggie caressed his forehead again, accompanied by a lilting "Shh, shh." He closed his eyes and sunk into her ministrations.

When he awoke, the sun was just beginning to set. They had mayhap an hour until dinner. Maggie was asleep next to him, her arm around his waist.

Propriety be damned, he rolled over and gathered her close, pressing his lips to her forehead.

"Callum," she said, her voice low and hesitant.

If she hadn't sunk deeper into him, he would have moved away. But she had, and her slender hand rubbed his back.

"Shhh," he whispered. "Supper will be soon. Just a few moments. Please."

"Okay," she whispered.

It took considerable restraint on his part not to kiss her then. He contented himself instead by pressing his lips back where they'd been on her forehead, feeling the warmth of her skin beneath.

'Twas a delightful interlude, this embrace betwixt them. A first while Maggie was awake and not caught in her disturbed slumber.

Long moments later, Anna knocked upon his door. She'd prepared a hot bath for Maggie in her chamber, and water was being dispensed for him as well.

Shifting to rise, he realized she had fallen back to sleep. He was tempted to leave her be. She looked so lovely and at peace there. But he knew how much she would enjoy a soak in a hot tub. Especially after their foray into the frigid waters by the lodge.

For a moment he imagined what it might be like to do so with her. To have her naked body lean back against his and loll as such. Shaking such thoughts from his head— *not now, Callum*—he rubbed his lips across her forehead one last time and softly called her name. She burrowed in closer and held him tighter for a second before startling awake.

"Are you okay?" She asked, cupping the side of his face.

He gave a nod and moved the hair fallen around her face back over her shoulder. "Anna called. It seems a hot bath awaits you, in your chamber."

"That sounds wonderful," she said with a sleepy smile. "Will you be alright?"

"I assure you, I'm fine. Anna will make sure of it. My own hot soak is on its way."

Maggie gave him one more concerned look before nodding and exiting the room.

A short time later, as he lay his head against the wooden rim of the tub, he heard a rap upon his door.

"Enter," he said, daring to hope it might be Maggie back again.

Grey came in holding his daughter, who was busy playing with her own feet.

"How's your head?" He asked.

"Better." Callum said, trying to hide his disappointment.

The baby reached out. "Um, Um." She said, her name for him. Callum smiled, and reached toward her, tickling her feet, which made her crow with laughter.

"When he's out of the tub, sweet." Grey told her. Callum closed his eyes again. In truth, fully relaxed and happy to be here again. Head wound and all. "Gwen approves whole heartedly of Maggie." Grey continued, and Callum let himself smile at the image. "She's told me they've bonded already."

"'Tis good to hear. Though I imagined they'd get on well." Callum replied, sinking further into the hot water. He didn't need Grey and Gwen's approval. However, having it made things easier.

Another hurdle crossed.

He wasn't sure when he began marking things off this imaginary list. As if he'd begun mapping out a strategy he only now realized necessary.

He didn't see Maggie again until just before supper. He waited on a bench in the hallway, ready to lead the way to the dining room. When she appeared outside of her chamber, he stood at once.

God's bones, she looked lovely.

She'd pulled her hair back and must have gotten a hold of what Gwen called her make-up. Her pretty eyes were darker, smoky and sultry and her rosy lips shined. She was also wearing his favorite sapphire blue dress. Fitting.

He took her hand, bringing it to his lips. "You look resplendent."

She smiled. "Gwen made an unexpected visit while I was getting ready, bearing some ointments and powders."

"I heard you two have become fast friends." He extended his arm, and she looped her own around it.

She stopped him atop the landing and looked out through the window to the sea. "I didn't have time earlier to savor this view, it's so lovely."

Maggie was right, 'twas a lovely spot. The view incredible. But her profile, framed by her soft cascading hair had his attention more so.

"Tell me of Seagrave. You seem very familiar with it." Maggie said as they reached the foyer.

"My friendship with Grey goes back to when we were just boys. Our parents were dear friends. Although there is an age difference betwixt us, Grey and I grew up as peers."

"How nice to have that connection with him."

"'Tis why I found myself here." He paused a moment before adding, "Some months after Fiona passed." Surely one must be able to speak the truth, even a painful one in close company.

She stopped and turned to him again, as she always did while engaged in a conversation of importance. Her head tilting but slightly as she looked up at him.

"I understand," she said. Her eyes locked onto his. "If I hadn't had Celeste, I'm not sure what I would have done.

It's hard to be alone. Especially after that period of time you prefer to be alone."

Callum nodded, knowing she was sharing something deep and personal just then. She rarely spoke of Celeste. From her previous stories, he knew her to be a great friend to Maggie.

"You should write her," he said. "She is welcome any time, Maggie. For as long as you both should like."

Something indescribable passed through her eyes before she closed them. "What I wouldn't give to see her again."

He pulled her in close, hoping to dispel this sadness he sensed so strongly in her. "We will make it so, I promise." If he had to travel himself to fetch her, he would. Better yet, he'd send someone.

Anything to make Maggie happy.

She gave a small sad smile, then reached up to run her delicate fingers across his forehead, down his temple and over his scar. He quivered at the sensation, as he always did. She lingered there for a moment tracing it, then shook her head and whispered. "What are we doing, Callum? I don't think—"

"Shh, think not." He wasn't absolutely sure himself. But he was not ready for her to put a name upon it or stop whatever this was betwixt them. He had serious doubt that could even be done. "We needn't do anything presently. Let's enjoy our time here and let the rest sort itself out."

He looked at the leather thong hanging about her neck and realized suddenly Gwen wore one too. Callum smiled at the symbolism of it. Emboldened, he reached out and fingered the leather, his hand brushing across the neckline of her dress. Which, luckily for both of them, was cut on the modest side. Still, his breaths quickened, and locking his eyes on Maggie's, he could tell hers did, too. Tracing his fingers along the leather, back up toward her neck, she covered his hand with hers, flattening it against her chest as she shivered. Her heart beat furiously, her lips slightly open.

Aye, he felt it too. Merely a second ago he'd meant to take her into the Great Hall, but now, he pulled her in close with his free arm, frozen to the spot.

He didn't wait for an invitation. Aye, the invitation was there in her eyes, and in her grip. In one swift motion, he covered her lips, drawing upon them lightly. God's bones, he felt it from the top of his head to the soles of his feet.

This pull, this attraction, this... Connection.

She moaned softly against him, releasing his hand and swept her fingers into his hair as he canted her head just so. Right there in the heart of the Seagrave's entrance they shared their first true kiss. He would remember it for always.

'Twas consequential.

Somehow, he heard Grey clear his throat. Putting up his hand to his friend, he drew upon Maggie's lips one last time before pulling away. She blushed when he looked at her, and almost immediately started shaking her pretty head.

"I don't think that helped," she said with a trill of laughter.

"Well, it surely did not hurt," he rasped, his thumb brushing the side of her face.

She rolled her eyes. "I meant—"

He shook his head, signaling her to stop right there. She did.

"Maggie of Sinclair," he said firmly. "May we let this be. Please. Let's enjoy supper. I promise you grand company and outstanding fare."

"We have that already, Callum." She said, reaching up to wipe what he assumed was some of the ointment he'd kissed from her lips.

"Then consider this a special treat."

"That's enough you two." Gwen called from the Great Hall. She was pouring wine, her favorite sport. "I think tonight calls for a celebration."

"You think everything calls for celebration," he and Grey said at the same time.

Maggie laughed then, a true laugh that lit her entire face. 'Twas similar to how she looked yesterday when she was pointing to the rabbits, and his heart constricted a bit at the thought.

How was that only a mere day ago, he wondered. It felt like nigh on a lifetime had passed since then. For once, well, mayhap more than once, he reached gratefully for the beaker Gwen extended his way.

Aye, a night of revelry was in order. He couldn't remember the last as such.

They sat before the fireplace and enjoyed a few morsels while he caught up with Grey and Gwen on family. Maggie moved to the floor next to the low table centered in the seating area, small plate in hand, selecting a few more tidbits.

He chuckled. "You'd think I don't feed you at Dunhill."

She looked up and beamed, then blushed. "This is usually my favorite part of dinner, it reminds me of home," she said covering her mouth.

"I'll inform Ide upon our return." He laughed again, a bit warm from the drink and company. He realized then he hadn't been happy here for some years. Seagrave had reminded him too much of the months after Fiona's death.

Now that changed.

To be honest, the happiness he felt now was different than what he'd felt with Fiona. Maggie, in her way, had changed him. Callum realized happiness was something to grab at, to strive for. Who knew what fate would throw his way?

Or, take away.

Cook came in then followed by her staff and they moved to the dinner table. He extended his hand to Maggie and pulled her up. The drink made them both giddy. When she stumbled into his chest, he had to stop short of pulling her in for another deep kiss, and settled for a light touch of his lips to her forehead.

Dinners at Seagrave were some of the best. The formality, as well as the food. And by formality he meant dinner was an occasion, treated as ceremony, to simply be together, not of pomp and circumstance. A time when everyone checked in with each other, no matter the business of the day. It was observed sacredly.

Greylen sat at the head of the table with Gwen to his left. Callum put Maggie on the other side next to Greylen then sat beside her.

"Don't you want to sit here?" She asked, as she took the seat next to Greylen.

"He doesn't want you to be left out." Gwen explained.

Leaving her on the end was not an option.

Maggie belonged in the center.

They commenced to have the night of merrymaking he'd envisioned. Gwen served his favorites, and he wasn't surprised to find Maggie liked them as well. He'd noticed they had similar tastes when it came to food. In fact, he told her not to get her hopes up. He had every intention of finishing every last morsel.

She made another sound of pleasure when she took her second bite of steak. "Is this zip sauce?" She asked Gwen, and Callum gave her a quizzical look. *What* sauce?

Gwen snorted and took another sip of her drink.

"Okay, that's enough for you." Greylen said with a laugh.

They played a game of team chess afterward. Callum minded not one bit, any of Maggie's moves on their behalf. She was an accomplished player already. Still, they lost. Grey and Gwen were worthy opponents. They all headed up the stairs together, Grey and Gwen turning one way while he and Maggie turned the other.

Alone together for the first time since their kiss, Callum felt his heartbeat pick up. Maggie, stared at him, leaning against the wall outside of her bedroom door, the shoes she'd discarded some time ago in one hand. He moved toward her, the heat between them felt nigh on scorching.

"That was one of the nicest evenings I can remember, Callum." Maggie breathed, after a moment. "Thank you for bringing me here."

Callum thought better of kissing her again. The night was perfect as is.

Even better when she cried out in her sleep sometime later. He padded down the hall, and into her room, gathering her close. She burrowed right against him and they slept soundly the rest of the night.

❧CHAPTER TWENTY❧

Maggie awoke earlier than usual the next morning. When she stepped into the hallway to see what roused her, she spotted Gwen starting down the stairs, baby in her arms. She was barefoot, in a robe. If Maggie hadn't known better, she would have sworn they were back in twenty-first century America.

Turning at the sound of Maggie's door opening, Gwen told her to grab the robe she'd left for her inside the bathing chamber and follow her. Eager to spend time with her new friend, Maggie did as instructed.

Padding after Gwen down the stairs, Maggie was surprised when they passed the Great Hall and headed toward the back of the keep. Gwen said hello to the staff, pointed out "Cook," though it's not like Maggie could have forgotten her. Last night's meal was sublime. Gwen gestured to a small table tucked off to the side, which was covered with a pretty linen runner, topped with a vase of fresh flowers. Beside the table, an open hutch displayed dishes and utensils, similar to the set up at Dunhill. Maggie smiled, remembering Callum had told her the idea had originated with Gwen.

Cook set a bowl of porridge or something of the sort down in front of Gwen. It was still steaming. She stirred it a few times before pushing it off to the side. Another girl appeared with fresh cream and a pot of what Maggie swore was... *no*.

She inhaled deeply again.

"Is that coffee?" She asked.

Gwen shot her a grin. "You miss it, don't you? And yes, it's really good too." Gwen poured them both a cup, took a sip of hers and sighed contentedly, then nodded Cook's way. "That woman knows what she's doing." Cook raised the utensil in her hand in acknowledgement.

Maggie followed suit, taking a deep sip from her mug. She let the brew course through her for a moment before turning to Gwen. "Oh, my God, this is so good. I haven't had a cup of coffee in over two years."

Gwen just smiled broadly and took another sip of her own. They sat there quietly for a few minutes, doing that coming to life stare while taking in the bustle in the busy kitchen. Finally, Gwen put her coffee down, one elbow on the table since the baby was still resting on her shoulder and said. "Okay. Story time. Give."

"I don't even know where to start."

"Well, when it was me, I had dreams of Greylen every night for five years. This is before I arrived here. Not that I ever saw his face or knew who he was, but it was *him*, you know?"

Maggie nodded, though this sounded nothing like what had happened to her.

"Anyway, after a while something just snapped, and I had to do something. So, I left my job, walked out on a contract, and took a trip to Scotland. Like I was pulled there or something. Four days later, on my birthday, I was caught in a storm and ended up in the water—and a few hundred years in the past."

"So, we're not doing the slow reveal?" Maggie said, and Gwen chuckled. "Okay, okay. Here's what I know. My boyfriend died—"

"Oh, Maggie, I'm so sorry." Gwen said, taking her hand.

"Thank you, it's okay now." Maggie shrugged. "I think."

Pausing again, Maggie looked off to the side, out the little window that overlooked a beautiful garden. It was so odd to have said that. Was it okay now? Strangely, it felt like it was.

She took a deep breath and turned back to Gwen, realizing aside from Celeste, who was combatting her own grief about Derek, she'd never talked about him or what had happened, like this, with a girlfriend. Even her conversations with Callum were different. Gwen was a true contemporary. Maggie knew implicitly she could speak freely about the how and why of it. Something she couldn't do with Callum.

"So many things have happened since. Back then, I was... shattered. I was a mess." Maggie said, grateful Gwen had given her the space to gather herself.

"What happened?"

Maggie swallowed hard and took another sip of coffee. "We were both detectives. We'd just closed a case and were off to celebrate—you know, dinner at the little Italian restaurant down the street. They had the best chicken marsala... and pizza. Anyway, we were on our way home for a quick change but stopped at the store for... for..." Maggie shook her head, and when she looked up at Gwen, she felt her chin start to wobble, and soon she couldn't see her through her tears. "It's so stupid. I wanted a candy bar."

"Oh, Maggie." Gwen came over to her, kneeling beside her. "You know it wasn't your fault, right? I'm sure you played the what if game a million times over by now, but I have to tell you—it's not your fault."

Maggie nodded. "I know," she said, gathering herself. "We were down the aisle when we heard the men come in. Typical robbery, God awful consequences." She let out a deep breath, "I haven't said that out loud. Ever. Not even to the department shrink. I'm not even sure I ever said that out loud to Celeste."

"Celeste?"

"Derek's sister, we were really close. Like, call ten times a day and come over every night close."

Gwen nodded and squeezed Maggie's hand.

"Soon after Derek was killed, Celeste told me she'd heard about this psychic who might be able to help with... I don't know what we thought, honestly. But I swear, Gwen, I pictured a witch who had a spell book and could bring him back."

"Like the two aunts in *Practical Magic*?" Gwen said, laughing a little.

Maggie pointed right at her, excited to find someone who would understand her references. "Exactly! I was desperate for anything but the scary redux of that boyfriend."

"So? Did you go?"

"I'm here, aren't I?" Maggie said dryly and Gwen laughed again. After telling her the rest of the story—the old bat's glowing eyes, the picture of Derek, the jewel, the sword, all of it—Gwen just stared at her for a moment before responding.

"Okay, wait," she said after a moment. "So, you landed outside of the Abbey—that part I get, but how did you come to be with Callum?"

"His aunt is one of the Sisters. I swear, Gwen, she took one look at me, crazy lady waving my phone in the air, dragging a sword, and pulled me inside so fast my head spun. Here I thought she was going to slam the door in my face."

"I had my phone too," Gwen said. "Well, an old one I basically just used as an iPod. Thank God I used to carry battery packs in my bag. We blew through all five though, the first three went quick, the last two we savored."

"Oh my God," Maggie said. "Battery packs. I forgot about those. They have solar chargers now."

"Does yours work?" Gwen asked excitedly.

"I... I haven't thought to try. I've kept it hidden."

"Well, you're obviously not going to get cell service, but the device itself should work if it has a charge. The camera, music, stuff like that." Gwen shrugged. "It's worth a shot."

Maggie started going through the possibilities when Greylen and Callum walked into the kitchen. Looking at them now with new eyes, she realized two things. One, they were similar in stature. Even if Grey had an inch or two on Callum, they were both well-built and plenty tall. And two, her heart ticked up more than a beat at just the sight of him. So at ease and light around his friends.

He caught her eye then and smiled, and God help her, she felt flush all over. That kiss last night in the foyer was an event. One she realized she'd been waiting for. It wasn't an all out make out fest, but the way he'd covered her lips. Well, it was beautiful and possessive all the same. Like *I've got you, and I've got this so just hold on.* Then he'd cupped her head and turned her just so, and went back in again. Thinking about it now, how he'd raised his hand to hold off Greylen and Gwen before nuzzling her and finishing with one last tug, she felt her blush deepen. Gwen must have noticed because she threw a linen napkin at her and laughed. Maggie chuckled and put her finger to her lips to shush her.

Greylen was holding his son, the toddler, and when they reached the table, he switched the older child for the baby in Gwen's arms. Gwen pressed her lips to the little boy's temple and whispered something in his ear, then reached for the porridge Cook left on the table, obviously the little boy's breakfast.

Cook came over with more coffee and what Maggie saw was basically a continental breakfast. She spied some delicious looking pastry, and a—wait, really? Quiche! Gwen must have taught Cook how to make quiche! Maggie chuckled at Gwen, who winked back.

"What's so funny?" Greylen asked.

"Maggie." Gwen said with a grin.

"Maggie of Sinclair, have you become a jester?" Callum teased.

The men settled and Callum brushed her arm with a murmur of "good morn," as if they did this every day. As if this wasn't a novel sensation. Maggie was struck by the intimacy of this moment.

Here they were, sitting at a small table in the corner of the kitchen, she and Gwen in their robes and Callum and Greylen in their fifteenth century versions of lounge wear. She reached out and fingered the material of Callum's shirt and breeches—yep, both were super soft. When she looked up again, everyone was staring at her.

She shrugged. "Sorry, I've never felt his night clothes."

"So you've felt his day clothes?" Greylen asked.

Maggie felt like she turned twelve shades of red. So, she liked to touch him, sue her. Callum was trying not to laugh, his cheeks a bit red too.

"Leave her alone." Gwen said, swatting at her husband.

"What of him?" Greylen asked, motioning with his head toward Callum.

"Oh, he's fair game."

Maggie put a hand on Callum's arm. "Oh, go easy on him. He's had a rough few days."

Greylen arched his eyebrow, filling their cups. Callum just grinned as he reached to grab plates and started passing them around.

"Father Michael will be here on the morrow." Greylen said, changing the subject.

The name rang a bell and Maggie thought back to Callum's confusion when she'd told him of her own Michaels family. "Father Michael?" She asked. "Your priest? I would love to meet him."

"Oh, I'd assume so," Greylen said with a smile that implied something more. "Obviously, you two will want some time with him." He paused, but Maggie had no idea what he meant. "He's been away this last week but is due to return. Timely, wouldn't you say?" Greylen finished pointedly, turning to Callum, who narrowed his eyes.

Maggie stiffened, feeling something was going on here, but didn't know what.

"Why?" She asked, at the same time as Callum.

Gwen covered her son's ears and leaned forward. "I mean, he *does* sleep with you, right? It's the fifteenth century, Maggie, not the twenty-first. There are certain customs you really should abide by, for everyone's sake."

Oh. *OH.* Maggie, wide-eyed, shook her head at Gwen, trying desperately to silently communicate with her *no, no, Callum doesn't know.* The last thing she wanted to do was ruin things between them. No matter how smart or 'free thinking' Gwen claimed he might be, she wasn't sure Callum would accept her if he knew that particular truth.

Then it hit her. Neither Greylen *nor* Callum seemed shocked at all by Gwen's mention of the twenty-first century. In fact, they were both just looking at her expectantly, almost placid.

"Wait, does he... know? About where you're from?" Maggie asked Gwen.

Gwen nodded, her eyes darting between the two men, who were doing the same.

"Know *what* about Gwen?" Callum asked with a practiced innocence Maggie could spot a mile away.

"Aye, pray tell, what?" Greylen demanded, shooting his wife another look.

"Oh, stop it you two." Gwen said with an exasperated sigh. "Maggie is... well, Maggie is—" Gwen glanced at Maggie, clearly trying to draw it out of her, tilting her head from left to right, but Maggie was *so* not going there.

No dice, amiga.

"Maggie is what?" Callum asked, covering her hand protectively, and Maggie's heart melted a little... more. He didn't know what secrets she was keeping from him. Yet here he was. *Poor Callum.* He curled his fingers beneath her palm, obviously anxious for what might come next.

Unable to stand it any longer, Maggie gave Gwen a firm nod. *Go on, spill, Gwen.*

"Maggie is like me."

"Like you... How?" Callum and Greylen asked together, leaning in toward Gwen like it would help her answer better.

Gwen leaned in. "She's from my time," she whispered. Then, lowering her voice even more, "the future."

Maggie wanted to crawl into a hole, or under a rock, anything at the moment. Surely, this would be too much for Callum to handle. Or he'd think she was crazy, or... She waited for the explosion... and waited... until—

"I knew it!" Greylen crowed, slapping his hand on the table, startling Maggie. "I asked you *last* night, *and* this morning," he chided. "And you said nothing."

"It wasn't my secret to tell." Gwen said, shrugging her shoulders.

Maggie nodded and offered a weak smile, waiting for Callum to say something.

Anything.

He was still holding her hand, but had begun staring at her in the oddest way. At first the expression made her nervous, but then she realized it wasn't horror or disgust, or even confusion. No, Callum was looking at her with, what she could only describe as, wonder.

"Callum?" She said, squeezing his hand. "Are you okay?"

He shook his head, as if coming out of trance. Then looked pointedly at each of them before staring directly into her eyes. "Glad tidings aside, Maggie of Sinclair," he rasped. His gaze almost hypnotic in its intensity. "I believe I am."

Maggie blushed under his stare, her heart pounding loudly in her chest. She had no idea what he meant by "glad tidings," but it included the word "glad," and that was enough for her right now. He wasn't put off by the fact she was from hundreds of years in the future.

Oddly, he seemed almost relieved by it.

"So, now that *that* business is taken care of," Greylen interjected, causing Maggie to startle. "You'll be wanting Father Michael to marry you when he arrives."

"*What*?" Maggie said. Is this how things were done in the fourteen hundreds? One kiss and you're locked together for life?

She whipped around to face Callum, who didn't seem fazed one iota. Greylen looked about to speak, but Gwen got there first.

"Well, you *are* sleeping together," Gwen repeated. "Right?"

"*Excuse me?*" Maggie choked out. She turned to face Callum who was reddening. A look of what might be realization crossing over his face.

"Maggie, let me explain." He said, and Maggie struggled to keep her composure.

"You told them about the lake?" She whispered, suddenly feeling... exposed... and... and *hurt*. They hadn't even discussed it.

It was sacred.

"Nae." He shook his head and grabbed her hand. The look on his face said it all. He knew it, too—it *was* sacred, and only between them. "I said nothing of the lake, Maggie."

"What happened at the lake?" Greylen and Gwen asked together.

"Wait," Maggie said, altogether confused now. "If Callum didn't tell you about that—which, by the way, was more of a life-saving-so-you-don't-freeze-to-death situation than anything scandalous—then what are you talking about? But, we're *not* sleeping together." *At least not yet*, she added to herself. At this point, Maggie had slept with just one person in her entire life.

Gwen gave her a smile and raised one eyebrow. "Are you sure, sweetie?"

Maggie shook her head, totally lost. She looked at Callum, who for once, wouldn't meet her gaze. Something started to bubble up inside Maggie—had he been spreading lies about her?

"Look," Gwen said, her face softening. "My husband can hear a pin drop on the other side of the castle. And according to him, you were crying out last night and Callum stopped by your room. I assure you, I heard no such thing." She made a drinking gesture with her hand. "I wasn't exactly in the most *observant* of states last night."

Maggie looked to Callum, questioningly. What was Gwen implying? Who was telling the truth?

"Oh, and besides, I saw him this morning when I went to fetch the baby. He was leaving your room." Gwen added.

Well, at least she knew what had awoken her so early this morning. It hadn't just been Gwen out in the hall. It was a small comfort, though, when the man she'd convinced herself was *actually* as good as she'd been told—who she'd begun to trust with her whole heart—seemed to be turning out to be anything but.

"Maggie," Callum rasped, and she whipped around to face him. "It's not what you think. You cry out in your sleep. I know you say you don't, but you do. You're desperate and terrified on those nights, tormented by visions I'm sure I can't myself imagine. I merely help you settle."

"You 'help me settle'?" Maggie quipped, feeling all eyes on her. "I'm curious, Callum," She twirled her hand for emphasis. "What does that look like?"

That gleam came back in his eyes, and she could tell he was trying not to smile. A flutter of frustration flared up in her, but she let him speak.

"Well the first time, I *did* try to wake you. But you flipped me on my back and had me pinned down—in truth, your move filled me with pride, but—" A wave of understanding passed over Maggie just as Gwen interjected.

"Ooh, nice move. Jiu Jitsu?" She asked eagerly. At Callum's withering stare, she merely shrugged. "Well, I think it's great Maggie was able to act defensively, and in her sleep no less."

From the looks Callum and Greylen passed her way, Maggie suspected there was a story there. She also started to suspect Callum might be telling the truth.

"Did I have your thumb pressed just so?" Maggie asked, displaying the odd angle she knew to be her go-to defense move.

He pointed at her. "Aye, that's the one. You came to your senses, *somewhat*, asked why I was there, *argued* when I told you, then settled yourself against me and fell fast asleep."

Maggie nodded, then leaned in and whispered. "How often has this happened?"

"We can hear you." Greylen and Gwen said, but Maggie shooed them off. She wanted an answer from Callum.

"A handful of times." He told her, taking a long sip of coffee.

"Whose handful, mine or yours."

He smiled and looked directly at her again. "Mine." He said, like a double entendre. And there it—*he*—was again, that possessive, warrior-like, heathen. Well, heathen might be a stretch, but this Callum took some getting used to.

"So," she said looking back at Greylen. "We're supposed to get married because he lays down next to me fully clothed sometimes?" She chose not to mention she was thinking about what would happen *without* so many clothes on.

Greylen rolled his eyes. "Are all women from the future daft, or is it simply you two? Regardless of what *happens* in that bed, you've shared it."

"Maggie doesn't believe in being wed." Callum said.

"Excuse me?" Came from Greylen.

Maggie shook her head, "It's not that I don't *believe* in it. It's just that with the last man, back in my own time, we never got around to it. It was more like a long—"

"Ten years." Callum interjected.

"Engagement." Maggie finished.

"They get around to it here," Gwen muttered. "Buckle up."

The baby started fussing then, thank goodness. Greylen and Gwen switched children again, then excused themselves. On her way out, Gwen told Maggie to take her time, but to meet her in the Great Hall once she dressed.

In the silence of the kitchen, after the MacGreggors left, Maggie and Callum brought their gazes to one another. Maggie took a steadying breath, wondering what would happen next, when Callum reached for her hand.

"Do we really need to talk to Father Michael?" She asked. The weight of what the MacGreggors had suggested settling on her now. "I mean, I don't want you to feel like you need to do such a thing. Not that you even *want* to. I don't want to be your problem or..." She trailed off, because what could she say? She *was* his problem, or at least his charge.

But to marry? Because of some misunderstanding? She'd just gotten used to the idea of caring for someone again.

Callum looked at her, so many emotions crossing his face. "You've never been my problem, Maggie." He said shaking his head. "But Gwen and Grey are correct. If I don't marry you, someone else will."

"Seriously?" Maggie balked. "You'd marry me just so no one else can? Romantic."

Something came over him then, his expression stunned, grief-stricken even. Maggie softened, looking at him. He remained silent for a long moment. Gazing out the little window by the table. When he finally turned back to her, he said, his voice gruff, "I never considered I would marry again." He took her hair and put it over her shoulder, which was now becoming a habit. "In truth, nothing of the sort ever crossed my mind. Until recently. Being *wed*, to *you*, Maggie of Sinclair, would be no obligation. As for someone else marrying you—'tis wholly unacceptable." He nodded then, as if done with the subject. "Come, I'll walk you back upstairs. Greylen and I have riding to do."

Well okay, then, Maggie thought. It's not like it would be a bad thing to be married to Callum. A good, principled man with whom she already felt a deep connection ... and, who she happened to be wildly attracted to.

"So, you're not upset about the other thing. With what Gwen said." Maggie was having a difficult time voicing it out loud herself.

"Grey and Gwen are two of the happiest people I know, Maggie."

"That doesn't mean—"

He put a finger to her lips and smiled, shushing her. "There's only one thing I know presently, Maggie of Sinclair." He said no more, leaving her to wonder, but took her hand, latching their fingers together.

It felt good to hold hands and walk beside him. The ever-present Callum-induced butterflies in her stomach had not subsided. There was always this constant hum beneath the surface when she was with him. But when she was next to him it felt magnified.

The castle was slowly coming to life as servants began their duties. Outside her chamber door, she turned to say... something... goodbye... see you in bit... Honestly, she wasn't sure. Callum had a look in his eye, and suddenly he was so close she could see the bright flecks in his deep blue eyes.

Feel the heat from his body.

Knowing what was coming, she wrapped her arms around his neck, shivering when he whispered, "Back to that one thing I know—I'm going to kiss you now, Maggie. Soundly."

She made an unintelligible sound. Her last thought as he leaned in and did what he'd said was *she might swoon from the pleasure of it.*

❧CHAPTER TWENTY-ONE❧

Callum pressed his body fully against Maggie. His physical attraction to her was nigh on transcendent, his senses strung tighter than a harp's cord in a constant state of reverberation. He knew she felt it, too. Her soft, panting breaths gave her away.

This was nothing like holding her at the lodge, or even at night when they slept. Both seemed wholly chaste in retrospect. Now, they were fully awake and completely engaged in this moment. With their first kiss behind them, any pretense of uncertainty was gone. He knew more of her, and she of him than any other. All their secrets laid bare.

They were bound together.

He nudged her with his face, rubbing his skin against hers, whispering in her ear. When she shivered against him, he groaned and fully embraced her turning her at just the right angle to cover her mouth. He couldn't recall experiencing a kiss as frenzied as this. When he tilted her head to the other side, he found entrance and took the kiss deeper. Roused by a loud noise, he pulled back. They stared at each other, wide eyed and out of breath, Maggie's fair lips swollen.

"Get a room." Gwen muttered walking by.

He and Maggie chuckled. Shaking his head, he ran a finger down the side of her face and lifted her chin to kiss her one last time. Chastely. Almost.

"I'm with Grey, today. You'll be alright?"

At her nod, he opened the door behind her, and waited for her to go inside. He stayed a moment, head pressed to the wood, feeling like a boy who needed to calm down.

He thought about Maggie's reluctance to marry as he made his way back to his chamber. They'd never spoken of marriage, but why would they have? It wasn't as if he'd been looking for a wife, or she a husband.

He hadn't met her by chance and was now wooing her. It—*she*—snuck up on him over the course of their time together at Dunhill. He was being honest when he told her he never thought to take another wife. More so, he never once thought of being with another woman.

Ever.

He wasn't sure if that was normal, but he'd taken a blow so fierce it felled him. Profoundly.

Then Maggie came along.

Thinking back, he wondered what would have happened had he answered his aunt's pleas to offer Maggie sanctuary from the first. He felt badly he'd denied the request and wondered if she'd suffered more from it. Then again, if she had been brought here from Gwen's future, perhaps the timing was all meant to be, and it wouldn't have worked out any other way.

Callum finished dressing in his riding clothes, with one thing he knew for certain on his mind. He needed to wed her and quickly. It was one thing to be cloistered far to the north at Dunhill. Another to be here at Seagrave, amongst so many other men who would have her if given the slightest chance.

What a fool he'd been. It had been his idea to bring her. He thought better of it then, and amended his previous thought. Mayhap, bringing Maggie with him, here, was exactly what he'd needed to do. It made him see their situation with clarity.

Making his way to the stables he thought of the time he'd spent here at Seagrave just after Fiona's passing. He'd ridden into the courtyard that first day and Grey had told him to put his horse away and clean up for supper, no questions asked. Gwen put him in the first room on the left, atop the stairs and embraced him as family. He'd seen firsthand, day in and day out, despite Grey and Gwen's differences, they were bound by love. Deeply.

Now Maggie had been affected by Seagrave, too. To hear tell of her coming from the future made her all the more fascinating. Is that why he found her so intriguing? Because she was like Gwen?

No. It wasn't that.

In fact, oddly, he hadn't seen anything in Maggie that shouted she was from the future. Mayhap it was the time she'd spent at the Abbey with his aunt. Or perhaps she just *fit* here. He liked that idea.

When he thought of Maggie, he thought of her smile, her eyes, the way she delighted over Ide's tea each morning. All the little things she did that made her, her. How she drew her bottom lip between her teeth when deep in a game of jacks, or how she tapped her finger against her chin when they played chess. The fierce look in her eyes as she narrowed them while she trained with her sword.

He kept busy with Grey until late in the afternoon. Maggie a constant on his mind. He waited for her again before supper, on the bench in the hallway, as had quickly become their habit.

She looked as lovely as the night before.

Her dress was a deep burgundy. She wore her hair down, her eyes and lips enhanced with make-up. When he asked of her day with Gwen, she broke out into a broad smile, placed her hand over her heart and thanked him for bringing her here. Then she'd looped her hand through his arm and began listing all of the things they'd done.

It felt good to listen to her tales of the day. He looked forward to introducing her to Lady Madelyn and hoped Greylen's mother hadn't been delayed yet again.

Callum and Maggie crossed through the threshold of the Great Hall just as Greylen entered from the other direction. He held Callum's sword out to him, a signifier his mandated two days of no swordplay were done.

"Stop misplacing this." Grey said with a grin before leaving Callum and Maggie be.

Callum foisted the weapon in the air, testing his arm, enjoying the weight in his hand. The other sword he'd been using was a fine replacement. But *this* sword, well, this felt like home.

When he brought it back down, he tilted it just so, showing Maggie the family crest and his initials he'd forged next to his father's.

"What was his name?" Maggie asked, fingering the letters.

"Ah." Having drawn her attention, she looked up at him and they shared a smile. "The mighty Fergus Donnan O'Roarke."

"A name I've not heard said in years," a voice called from above.

Callum turned to see Lady Madelyn descending the stairs and bowed his head. "Forgive me, Lady Madelyn. Had I known you were on your way down I would have accompanied you as well."

"Oh, nonsense," she said, stopping before him and swatting his chest, much like his aunt would do. Of course, Lady Madelyn was as much an aunt to him as could be, without the blood relation. She kissed each of his cheeks and smiled a moment longer than necessary. 'Twas always like this after a time of not seeing each other. As if just being in each other's presence made them reminiscent of years past. "I still miss her." She said of his mother. "Your eyes remind me of her, each time I see you. Now tell me." She said looking at Maggie, "Who is this lovely creature you have with you?"

"Lady Madelyn, may I present Margaret Sinclair."

"Maggie, please," she said with a curtsy. It struck him then, Gwen never curtsied. He wondered if Maggie had learned that at the Abbey. "We were just admiring Callum's sword and the lettering between the jewel and the crest."

"I'm so pleased you've recovered your sword, Callum. I remember you'd lost it some time ago." Lady Madelyn looked down to the spot Maggie had pointed out and gasped. "Wait!" she cried, stumbling in her haste, causing Gwen and Greylen both great alarm as they rushed to her side.

She waved them off but was still herded by her son and daughter-in-law to a large armchair. "I'm fine." She argued, swatting them away. "The sword. Callum," she said, reaching out. "Please bring it to me."

Callum did as she asked, laying it across her lap and kneeling beside her. She touched the jewel and looked up at the ceiling, "Oh, Isabeau."

"Lady Madelyn?" Callum was confused at her display. "What is it?"

"'Tis the stone, Callum." Her eyes were gleaming, and she laughed softly. "I was there... I was there."

She trailed off for a moment, as if getting lost in her own memories and Callum felt his heart race, wondering what she knew.

"You know of the stone?" He could only imagine what his wide-eyed marvelment appeared like to the others. God's bone's, her account added credence to the tale his aunt had told.

For all of his life, no one ever mentioned the stone's absence *or* existence.

And now in two months it seemed his life suddenly revolved around it.

"Oh, Callum, of course I know of the stone." She smiled at him then, much like his mother would do, and God help him if he wasn't overcome with a sensation that ran through his entire body. "I was there, at the festival that night. The night your mother removed it from your father's sword."

It was one thing to hear the story from his aunt, quite another to hear tell of it from Lady Madelyn. Especially considering how Greylen and Gwen were brought together. It was becoming more and more difficult to discount it for whimsy or coincidence.

"I didn't know you were there. My aunt didn't say," Callum said, fixing Lady Madelyn with an intense stare.

"Oh, we always attended together. Alistair and your father set up our tents right next to each other."

Callum had fond memories of the festival. Yet somehow it had escaped him, that his parents and Grey's would have attended together so long ago. Grey pulled some chairs forward, and they gathered around leaning in to hang on her every word.

She told it all, how his mother shared with his aunt and Lady Madelyn her wish for him, her unborn babe at the time. The price the woman demanded for such, and how they'd laid chase to find the mysterious enchantress the next morn.

"Did you know the woman? The one who my mother gave the sapphire to?"

Lady Madelyn nodded. "Aye, 'tis the same woman who foretold the prophecy of Greylen and Gwendolyn.

So, you can see," she said, with a nod to Maggie. "Why I'm so curious about all of this."

God's bones.

Could Maggie be his Gwen?

In truth?

He laid a hand on her leg, and looked at her. She'd been silent until this moment but now leaned forward.

"Prophecy?" She asked.

Grey stood, always eager to take center stage when he could, and began the recitation. He'd done so nigh on a hundred times at last count.

"To the Greatest Highland Clan—" he boomed, but stopped when Maggie broke in with a small yelp.

They both whirled round in alarm at the sound of her voice, and saw her stricken look and pale face. She spoke then, her voice barely above a whisper. "A doctor... a detective—"

Suddenly, Maggie crumpled forward. His arm braced her before she fell to the floor and he pressed her back into the chair. Taking care to push her hair back, before stroking her face in hopes to bring her out of her swoon.

When she opened her eyes, he told her, "You fainted."

"I don't faint," she said.

"Of course you don't. You don't cry out in your sleep either," he muttered, rolling his eyes. Then he stepped aside, nodding to Gwen for her inspection.

"Wait," Maggie said, her voice insistent. She grabbed Gwen's arm. "Are you a—" She looked around then at everyone in the room, then lowered her voice again. "A doctor?"

Gwen gave her a small smile. "Aye, Maggie, I am. Don't worry though, it's not a secret here, and definitely not in present company." She chuckled and winked a second before saying, "We have a saying here, don't we boys?"

He and Grey delivered it on cue. "What happens at Seagrave, stays at Seagrave."

Maggie's eyes darted to him. "Oh my God, is that supposed to be a joke?" She suddenly looked worse than before. "I think I'm in some weird alternate reality movie," she whispered to Gwen.

"Let's give her a little bit of space, okay?" Gwen said.

Callum ignored Gwen's wishes and set her out of the way, kneeling again before Maggie.

"Hey." Gwen cried, swatting his arm. "I mean it, Callum. This has all been an incredible shock for her."

"For me as well," he snapped, at the moment feeling impulsively protective. He saw Grey hold up his hand and craned his head in time to see Cook and her staff retreat. They'd gone from heady enjoyment to fraught intensity in a blink of an eye. Maggie still looked frightful... mayhap ill... God's bones... suffice it to say, she didn't look well.

"Why don't we take a few minutes, to calm down?" Gwen said. "Cook will be back soon. Once dinner is on the table we can resume where we left off." She pushed a glass in his hand then and snapped, "Water. For Maggie." Callum had to admit, to himself, not to Gwen, he deserved her ire.

He lifted it to Maggie's lips, and she drank obediently. "I'm okay, really." She said after a few scant sips. She whispered then, "You're rubbing my leg."

"We can hear you." Grey and Gwen chimed.

Maggie chuckled, a bit of color coming to her face. He breathed a sigh of relief. Considering her spell just moments ago, he decided not to tell her—yet—come the morrow it would not matter that he rubbed her leg in plain view.

They must be wed.

"I think this calls for a brandy," Gwen called from the other side of the room, not knowing just how celebratory Callum's thoughts were.

"You think everything calls for a brandy," he and Grey said in unison.

Maggie chuckled again, and when he gave her an inquisitive look, she nodded. "I'm better. I swear."

Servants came in then with dinner, and they busied themselves with finding places at the table. Grey at the head, he and Maggie on one side, and Gwen and Lady Madelyn on the other.

"Mother, why don't you finish telling us about the fair?" Greylen said once they'd been served.

"Wait," Maggie interjected. "If I may, please. In my shock, I almost forgot. Would someone tell me about the prophecy? I still don't understand what it is or what it's about."

They all looked at each other. A silent duel of who would give first and offer the explanation. Then they all spoke at once. For a moment, a commotion broke out. In deference, he, Grey, and Gwen bowed to Lady Madelyn.

"Ah, the prophecy," she began. "You see, dear. The prophecy is the enchantment that foretold us Greylen and

Gwendolyn were fated to be together. 'Twas foretold by the very same woman who Isabeau gave the jewel too. To pay her for her services."

"That's why Greylen wasn't totally freaked out I was from another time," Gwen supplied with a shrug. "It was written in the prophecy."

Callum remembered Greylen telling him of the prophecy some years ago. Still, when he'd first met Gwen, he'd been quite leery. It took some time for him to be a staunch believer, but the more he was around her, the more sense it made.

"You believe in all of this?" Maggie asked, shaking her head and looking bewildered.

"You're here, aren't you?" Gwen said pointedly. Then she patted her mother-in-law's hand and told her, "Maggie is from the future too, mother."

"Oh my," Lady Madelyn exclaimed. "Maggie, how did you to come to be here?"

"That's a question I used to ask myself all the time." Maggie said, shaking her head.

"Used to?" Gwen said.

Callum took note as well. Maggie shrugged. "Well, ever since coming to Dunhill, I suppose I stopped asking. But back then, when this all started, this woman gave me the stone. I'm starting to think she's the old ba—the same woman who told you about the prophecy, and who Callum's mother originally gave the stone to."

"What makes you think that?" Gwen asked.

"She had this small wooden chest and a thick ledger. She brought it out and started to recite—*verbatim*—what

Greylen did a few minutes ago when you spoke about the prophecy."

Maggie already had their attention, but at this, everyone's expression turned to astonishment. If Maggie thought she'd encountered this same woman centuries in the future, that would make her nigh on seven hundred years old.

"She recited the prophecy?" Gwen asked. "The same woman Lady Madelyn and Callum's mother knew from well over thirty years ago is the same woman you went to in *our time*? In the future?"

Maggie shrugged. "At this point, your guess is as good as mine. All I know is she said those words, gave me the sapphire, and told me not to let it go."

"I wonder if she'll be there come spring. Lady Madelyn?" Gwen asked, looking intrigued by the possibility.

"I suppose she might be," Lady Madelyn said. "We haven't been in years, but I did see her the last time Alister and I took Isabelle."

These revelations caught Callum completely unawares. Especially that Maggie had been given the stone first, separate from the sword. He'd never considered Maggie having one without the other. He'd assumed she'd come by the sword *with* the stone fixed in place.

"Maggie, how..." He started, but God's bones, he wasn't even sure what to ask. "This woman gave you the jewel, did she not give you the sword, too?"

"No, at the beginning, I only had the stone. I carried it with me every day for months." Maggie said. Her voice small and shaky, but growing stronger as she went on.

"I stumbled upon the sword one afternoon. It had been hidden, and I found it tied under our—my—bed. And when I sat there looking at that hollow beneath the wolf crest—"

"Little wolf," everyone at the table said together.

Maggie looked startled at their outburst but how could she know that their family crest had such meaning. *Little Wolf* was what his parents called him when he was a boy. Everyone knew this, everyone besides Maggie. Even Gwen had heard the stories when he'd stayed with them.

She had grown very quiet, a puzzled look on her face. Like she was working something out in her mind. She turned to him then, "Why did your mother give the old ba—give that woman the stone?"

He stared at her and had an ominous feeling the answer would not please her. He wasn't sure why, but suddenly it didn't feel like good magic was at hand.

"I was told she used it to pay for my soul's good keeping," Callum said after a moment.

"What does that mean?"

"She wanted Callum to have a grand love." Lady Madelyn said.

Maggie made a horrified face. "Are we supposed..." She gasped, "Do you think that's why they... they—"

God's bones. He knew what crossed her mind, he could feel it. *That* was not the reason Fiona and Derek died, he was sure of it.

"Nae!" He insisted, grabbing her hand. "We will go see her, this enchantress or mystic or witch or whatever she is for ourselves, and ask her directly."

Maggie stood, fanning herself, and began pacing. She looked terribly distraught, and he went to her in hopes of calming her down. His heart broke at the look she gave him, like they were responsible for something horrendous.

"I swear to you, Margaret Siobhan, what you are thinking is nigh on impossible."

"Are you sure?" She clutched him in her desperation. "Can you be sure whatever was done years ago didn't cause what happened to them so the stone would bring me to you?"

God's bone's, what was he supposed to say? "I swear it. On all that is Holy," he said for her sake.

He held her gaze until she seemed to accept his declaration as truth with a decisive nod. Maintaining his stance, he stayed with her as she slowly calmed, releasing his shirt from her grasp and smoothed the material across his chest. He led her back to the table where blessedly the subject everyone had, without a doubt overheard, went unmentioned.

Maggie took a sip of her brandy, laid her napkin across her lap and gave a small yet warm smile to the table at large.

"Are you ready to continue your story?" He asked, trying not to rush her, but eager to hear what had transpired.

"Where had we, had we... I'm sorry—"

"Do not fret," he said, covering her hand. "You were telling us you'd found the sword hidden under your bed."

"Oh, right. There's not much else, Callum." She said with a shrug. "I placed the stone in the hollow and... well here I am."

He and Grey exchanged a pointed look. Callum

nodded, "Tomorrow."

"Tomorrow, what?" Maggie asked.

"Tomorrow we'll wed."

Maggie started choking on her water. He patted her back until her fit subsided. "We're back to this?" She asked.

"Aye." Surprisingly he felt quite satisfied. Greylen had his Gwen. And now he had his Maggie, equally fated—or so he'd decided to believe.

He looked away for a moment and felt her sharp focused stare. Suddenly amused, he smirked to himself, took the rest of his drink, and like a smug cat that just swallowed a bird, turned his attention to her.

Fully to her.

One Maggie of Sinclair.

"That's all you have to say?" She asked.

"Aye." He told her pointedly.

"I told you," Gwen said.

Maggie looked aghast. For the life of him, he cared not a wit. What in the name of God had come over him? He could truly think of nothing presently but glad tidings. She might have said something then, but Callum was lost in his thoughts.

"Callum? Callum?" Maggie rubbed his arm. "Did you even hear one word I said?"

He made a subtle move with his head, cleared his thoughts, and gave her his undivided attention now. "Forgive me, no."

"Uh oh." Gwen said from across the table. He shot her look.

"Uh oh, what?" Maggie asked.

"That look." Gwen shook her head.

"That's enough, Gwen." Callum bit out.

"What about it?" Maggie asked, never taking her eyes off of him. When Gwen didn't answer, Maggie looked over at her. "Well?"

"You're toast."

Callum heard Gwen say this before. Usually when she was reprimanding Grey or one of the men. Or calling a move well played.

"I still don't understand why we have to get married. I mean, I get the whole we're sleeping together thing." Her eyes widened, and she turned to Grey's mother. "—Oh, Lady Madelyn, we're really not *sleeping* together. More like... beside one another."

Lady Madelyn covered her mouth with her hand, chuckling softly.

"The reason has not changed," Callum said firmly. "If I don't marry you, you will be considered fair game. Which I have said is wholly unacceptable. If we attend the festival and you are not spoken for, someone could take a liberty. And if anyone lays a hand on you. I. Will. Kill. Them."

Maggie's eyes grew wide.

"Why you didn't think of this before, I don't understand." Gwen interjected, adding tinder to the fire. "Even if you hadn't been sleeping together. It should have occurred to you, Callum."

"We're NOT sleeping together!" Maggie insisted.

"Aye, we are." Callum countered, quite enjoying seeing Maggie so riled up.

"You're not helping the situation, Callum."

"I am. I happen to be on the other side."

"Can't we call a draw on this one?"

"This is not an instance I would consider such." He took her hand. "Maggie, Gwen is correct. This should have occurred to me some time ago. I could lay a hundred reasons why it escaped me at your feet, but the fact remains. Now that we are here, and away from the privacy of Dunhill, there is no other choice."

"It's just so... so... It just doesn't make sense to me."

"Grey, please explain to Maggie so she will understand."

She looked at his friend then, a bit of expectant optimism in her eyes that he might deliver a palatable alternative.

"You're getting married." Grey said pointedly, destroying whatever flicker of hope she may have had.

"Please excuse me." She said to everyone save him.

He followed her upstairs and caught her outside her room. He knew he should let her be, but he couldn't. "Maggie."

"I'm confused, and tired. I just need some time, please."

He couldn't blame her, considering all that had occurred the last two days. He'd pushed enough and for now acquiesced.

Returning to the Great Hall, he grabbed the decanter and poured another round for Gwen, Greylen, and himself before sitting down. He chuckled when Gwen mouthed, "I love you." And gratefully took a deep sip from her cup.

"What now?" He asked to no one in particular.

"The choice is yours. Morning or afternoon?" Grey asked, referring to the time he and Maggie would be wed.

"Morning. Discreetly. Too many arriving in the afternoon. We'll wait for Dar and Ronan, they should be here early enough."

"Then it's settled. The Chapel?"

Gwen shook her head and rolled her eyes. "What part of all of us walking to the Chapel is discrete? I say we do it here, like right here in the Great Hall."

She was correct. Anything that involved the Seagrave courtyard, even a leisurely stroll of an intimate gathering of five would draw attention. 'Twas where most dramatic events occurred.

Case in point, his arrival with one Maggie of Sinclair.

Much later that night, his fair Maggie called out again. He padded down the hall and into her room, and got into bed beside her. Gathering her close, he shushed her, and she quieted almost at once as if used to his voice and the calm that followed once he arrived. He patted her hair down, tucking it beneath his chin, and fell asleep with thoughts about the morrow. Hoping the day would go without fanfare.

At least the part in which he wed Maggie.

CHAPTER TWENTY-TWO

Maggie awoke before the sun rose. Too much on her mind to keep her in bed. Staring out the window, she marveled at how she'd found herself on the verge of yet another life-changing event.

Another one she had no control over.

She'd been enjoying her budding relationship with Callum and how slowly and subtly things had been progressing. She never imagined having feelings for someone again. Actively avoided getting too close to new people. But it had snuck up on her, and she wasn't entirely upset about it. It's not that the idea of marrying Callum was so bad; after all, he was a good man. She was attracted to him, and she felt safe with him—he'd saved her life, for goodness sakes!

It doesn't get much safer.

What really bothered her was being told what to do, how, and when to do it. That they had to be married, *now*. That didn't sit right with her. She'd had little control over anything these past two years in this century—that is until Sister Cateline brought her to Dunhill.

At Dunhill she'd found a semblance of freedom. It started to feel like a new life was possible. Was that all coming to an end? Was her free will being threatened? Or, perhaps, was getting married to Callum the way to maintain it? He would be kind to her. She knew that. It just felt like she was losing whatever little power she had left.

Maggie heaved a sigh and leaned her forehead against the cool glass of the window.

With morning fast approaching, Maggie's attention turned to the courtyard, coming to life down below. Her view of the land was interrupted by Callum leaving the smithy, admiring something in his hand.

So, he'd been awake early too.

He was with two men she didn't recognize. She assumed they were Dar and Ronan. He'd told her they were expected to arrive early, the morning before the festival. Aidan, the last of their brotherhood, wouldn't make it until later. She'd been excited to meet them yesterday.

Today, she wasn't so sure.

She smiled despite herself as a young boy ran from the outbuilding Callum had just left. As only the young do, the boy hopped twice, landing with a jump before Callum. Callum reached out and ruffled the boy's hair, his large hand all but covering his entire small head. The boy placed his hands palms up in front of him, and Callum threw his head back and laughed.

Maggie wasn't sure what was so funny, but then Callum fished a pair of long thick gloves from his waistband, obviously smuggled from the smithy. Maggie added sticky fingers to her growing list of monikers for him. The boy beamed and ran off, turning to wave before disappearing into the smithy.

She knew Callum whittled and crafted with his hands. She had that beautiful elephant he'd made for his mother on her night table at Dunhill. But Maggie hadn't expected him to forge iron as well. Was this a hobby, too?

Whatever it was, she had to admit it was attractive. Then Maggie cursed herself and thought better of wondering *anything* of Mr. One-syllable-word, Sticky-finger, Insufferable, Overbearing, Warrior Callum O'Roarke.

She was trying to forget it all at the moment.

Maggie had been coming around to the idea of getting married until she'd felt forced into it.

They had all been quite plain with their insistence last night. Even Gwen. There was no other way than to wed. And at this point, Maggie was pretty sure she understood. It did make sense.

It *was* her best case scenario.

She'd just been so pissed off by Callum's smug look and Greylen's last remark, the way it had felt that they'd ganged up on her, she'd up and left. A kind servant girl had brought a tray with a fresh plate of food to her room shortly after she'd fled the Great Hall last night. While Maggie was touched by the kindness, her cheeks flamed, knowing surely the castle was abuzz with the latest gossip.

Down below, Maggie watched as Callum looked up to her window. Startled, she stepped back, hoping he hadn't seen her. She wasn't ready... for anything at the moment.

As if on cue, someone knocked on her door and she grabbed the robe she kept on the end of her bed. She'd learned over the last few days, you had to move quickly here at Seagrave if you wanted to keep up. Just as Maggie was belting it shut, Gwen opened the door, bearing a sympathetic smile and a cup of coffee.

"Want some?" She asked.

Maggie, somewhat heartened to see her new friend, took the bribe and waved her in. Anna followed, and set a large tray with her favorite breakfast items on the table in the seating area, while a few girls carried garments and accessories to the dressing area.

"May I?" Gwen asked, pointing to the sofa.

"Of course," Maggie said, taking a seat beside her.

Too overwhelmed and dejected to remain upright, she laid her head against the cushion. Gwen said nothing, but mimicked her position, so they were face to face, with their feet tucked up beneath them.

"I'm sorry about last night." Gwen said.

Maggie gave a tight smile. She wasn't sure how she felt. And frankly was beginning to wonder if it even mattered. "Thanks."

Gwen reached out to give Maggie's forehead a reassuring pat, like any good friend or mom or sister might. Her nurturing touch was Maggie's undoing, and she started to cry. At first, it was a few silent tears, but then the dam broke. Gwen said nothing, and just held her while she sobbed. Like an uncontrollable, shoulder wracking, nose running, gasping bawl fest.

Soon Maggie was crying, not just over last night, but releasing the buildup of *everything* that had happened. Honestly, she couldn't remember the last time she had a good cry. Her low spirts this morning and Gwen's ministrations had loosened something in her.

"Oh, sweetie." Gwen repeated over and over, rubbing her back now. At Gwen's beckon, Anna sat behind her so Maggie was enveloped in warmth.

It took a few minutes until Maggie calmed enough to pull away. When she did, still sniffling, Anna handed her a few linen squares, patted her on the back and returned to directing the servants who had appeared with steaming buckets of water. Maggie took one last deep, shuddering breath and wiped her face.

"Better?" Gwen asked.

Maggie shrugged. "I'm not sure." While the cry was a much needed release, she still felt things were moving way too fast and completely out of control. "Is there any oth—"

"Nae." Gwen shook her head. "This is the only way, Maggie. Let's say you don't marry Callum, and someone comes along and notices you. They think you're pretty— which you are, and you know it, so don't even try that with me. Anyway, this guy decides he wants you and since you're not married—don't *belong* to any man, so to speak—he takes you. Guys in this era aren't just going to get your number and text you at 2AM. Or follow you on social media and like all your pictures. They've got swords. They're used to just... taking. And that's that. Not that Callum won't find you and get you back. But by then, who knows what damage might be done. It's 1430 Maggie, and as I learned some time ago, we are *so* not in Kansas anymore."

"So, I should just be resigned to marry him?" She said glumly, finally getting the full picture.

"Callum." Gwen said.

"Duh, who else?"

Gwen stared at her, bug-eyed, motioned with her head, and mouthed, "Call-um!"

Oh.

Maggie whipped her head around to find him standing in her doorway. His face was impassive, but his eyes telegraphed concern.

"I heard you cr—I heard your distress and wanted to check on you." He said in explanation. He gave a curt nod to the room at large and left.

She scrambled off the sofa and ran after him. He moved quickly as any lithe, fit, large man would with his stride and was already partway inside his room when she caught up to him.

"Callum," she said, reaching out to him. "Please, let me explain."

"You needn't," he said without turning, pulling his shirt off over his head and casting it aside. "I will wed, honor, and protect you no matter your feelings."

He went deeper in his chamber and she followed him, admiring his broad back and trim waistline in spite of herself. She realized then she'd never seen him without a shirt. And my goodness, he put the guys she used to exercise next to at the gym to shame. His every muscle flexed with each step he took.

When he sat on a bench at the end of his bed, she almost tripped from the front view. His bare chest was a sight to behold, wide and impressively built. And his shoulders and arms, *well*. She caught herself then, and sobered immediately, devastated she hurt this man who never hurt her.

"Please, let me explain," she repeated, stopping him mid reach, and pulling his boots off herself before setting them aside. Still flustered, she moved on autopilot and pulled his socks off, too. Which, he let her do. He had startlingly nice feet. *Biiiigggg* feet.

She wondered for a second if what they said was true. Then got back to the problem at hand. "What you heard..." She said, standing between his legs, which had parted to allow her. "Was... I said it rhetorically." Maggie lifted his chin so she could look in his eyes and shrugged, hoping the sorrow she felt, that he'd overheard her careless remark was plain for him to see. "Being wed to you would not be a hardship. It's only that..." She looked away, trying to search for the right words. Then looked down at him again before continuing. "Please understand, Callum, not making my own decisions or even having the power to do so, is incredibly difficult. And scary."

"You haven't upset me, Maggie of Sinclair. In truth, I have much to thank you for. You've snapped me out of my melancholy and helped me return to the man I once was." He smirked then, that smug look with a devilish gleam in his eyes. "'Tis good to be back, lass."

"Well, this *new* you is going to have to work to be as charming as the old you." She told him. She started running her fingers through his hair absently with one hand, tracing his scar with the other. "*He's* going to have to work to win me over."

"Oh, *he* will, lass. You'd best get used to him, quickly though. *He's* going to be sharing your bed tonight."

With that, he stood. As he did so, his arm snaked around her back, undoing the sash that held her robe closed in one swift motion. The heat from his touch was nearly searing, with only her thin chemise as a barrier. Being engulfed by this new, more brazen Callum both startled and excited her.

His large hand upon her back pressed into her just firmly enough her breasts crushed against his bare chest. He stared deeply into her eyes as his hand fisted her hair, and leaned in slowly, building the anticipation for what she knew was inevitable.

The kiss was beautiful and gentle, poignant even at the start, but heated up quickly. If she'd had time to think, Maggie would have been embarrassed by her eagerness. Like some teenager necking behind the bleachers; she'd have to scold herself later for encouraging him. Scorching her nails across the back of his head, tugging and nipping him back, and yes using her tongue to duel with his.

It was as if he knew what her body would react to and followed suit with the exact moves that had her clinging to him and mewling like a god damned kitten. Her nipples were hard as rocks and the friction as he moved her slightly to the left and right was like a lightning bolt straight to her center. As moisture pooled between her legs, she cursed him, smiling despite herself. This attraction was so unfair. She was breathless when he set her down and surprised to find they were beside his bedroom door. She'd missed the journey, but the ride was fantastic.

He grinned at her, studying her face. Or maybe admiring the evidence of his ravishing. "Now if you'll excuse me, I have a ceremony to prepare for."

Then the heathen stood there waiting for her to leave. She made as dignified an exit as possible, but at the last moment stuck out her tongue.

CHAPTER TWENTY-THREE

"That man is a pig! An arrogant, archaic, neanderthal, pig!" Maggie huffed when she came back into her room.

"No truer words could be spoken." Gwen agreed with a nod, looking relieved she'd at least come back mad and not crying. "Caveman works well, too. Be careful, though. If you really are fated for one another, and it's anything like what happens between me and Greylen, this... chemistry can be explosive. Trust me. You'll fill up that castle in no time. But also enjoy every second of it." When Maggie rolled her eyes, Gwen shook her head fervently. "No, you don't understand, Maggie. If he's anything like Greylen, he'll play you like a violin and leave you weeping at his feet."

"That's just stupid, Gwen. They're from the fifteenth century," Maggie snapped. So, she went off a little. Maybe Gwen hit a nerve. "You're a smart woman. Get ahold of yourself."

Gwen gave her one of those *if you say so* looks and a shrug. "Remember when I told you these men were well schooled? I didn't just mean textbook smart. They've had a very well-rounded education."

"What does that mean?"

"I think part of their instruction included learning about women." She did an eyebrow dance. "Probably from the best paid courtesans of our—this—time."

Maggie rolled her eyes. But based on what just happened, it was possible.

"Just saying," Gwen finished.

Two hours later, Maggie was bathed, dressed, and coiffed. Her snit had subsided, and honestly, she was relieved she hadn't hurt Callum.

He didn't deserve that.

She'd been mortified he'd overheard what she'd said to Gwen. She decided to look at things logically and realistically. Callum's mom and Maggie's own complicity in spell conjuring or magic making aside.

This, her marriage to Callum, could be seen as an arrangement. A partnership. She wasn't in love with him. Though she'd been teetering on the edge just two days ago. For now she decided, she cared for him.

Deeply.

She was a rational adult and wanted to remain that way. Rational where Callum was concerned. Maggie did not want to give her heart away to lose it again later if, or when, something happened.

She couldn't.

She wouldn't.

But she could care for him, could be a loyal friend and confidante. They would be married because it was the sensible thing to do. Maggie could accept that, own that decision. But it was to be nothing more. Not that there wouldn't be more, physically.

Of that she was sure.

She remembered her mom telling her once, as Maggie was transitioning from tween to teen, how unpredictable hormones could be. At the time, Maggie rolled her eyes, deeply embarrassed her mother would even suggest such a thing. But now—she and Callum were a prime example of hormones-gone-wild.

Once she realized she could compartmentalize things and begin to use the logical part of her brain, which had kind of gone to the wayside since she'd taken up residence at Dunhill, Maggie actually had fun being fussed over in preparation for the ceremony.

Gwen brought in five dresses from her sister-in-law Isabelle's closet to choose from, in case Maggie didn't have anything in her own wardrobe she wanted to wear. Greylen's sister and her husband Gavin were supposed to come back with Lady Madelyn yesterday. But Isabelle was pregnant again and not feeling well, so Gavin insisted on staying behind with her and their little ones. Maggie still marveled at the thoughtfulness of the men in this circle.

Barbarians that they were.

She'd never pictured herself as one of those fairytale princess brides, anyway. So, she was fine with the selection she had to choose from. Pretty, classic dresses, but nothing too froufy.

Especially since this just didn't feel like a real wedding. Besides, it wasn't like they were having a grand ceremony and reception afterward. From what Gwen had told her, they'd kept the whole thing pretty hush-hush. Which was fine with Maggie. If she could, she'd like to skip it altogether. But of course, she couldn't.

So, Maggie steeled herself to be a big girl, and counted her blessings that if she had to get married, at least it was to Callum.

In the end she chose a fur-trimmed French inspired gown. It was a deep shade of burgundy with a V-neck that displayed her black kirtle and a band of her chemise. Wanting to make a statement, and begin this marriage on the right foot, Maggie asked Anna if she could fashion a tartan of Callum's clan into a cloak.

The deep green with soft shoots of blue and amber would complement her dress beautifully. And it only took a few stiches here and there to achieve the desired results.

When Gwen remarked on her sudden turn, Maggie shrugged. "I'm sure there are worse things than being married to Callum O'Roarke."

As she and Gwen entered the Great Hall some hours later, her back was straight and her chin up. With her decision to enter into this marriage, but on her own terms, Maggie managed to detach herself from what was happening, finding it easier to play her part.

The men were speaking to each other, and luckily their numbers had remained low. Callum, Greylen, and the two men she assumed to be Dar and Ronan, dressed formally. Maggie had to admit she loved Callum's outfit. His white shirt, black britches, and tall polished black Hessian boots.

He looked stupid good.

So good Maggie felt her resolve weaken. Even more so when he didn't take his eyes off her as she made her way through the room. Lady Madelyn was seated in a large armchair and when she started to get up, Maggie stayed her with what had to be her best regal curtsy to date. With little time to congratulate herself, Maggie approached the group of men. Callum separated himself and came to stand in front of her.

His close proximity threatened her resolve even further. When he reached for her hand, she had to look away briefly to regain herself.

"You look so beautiful, Maggie." He said in a low voice.

"I chose the dress with your mother in mind."

"She would approve. Too, of my tartan."

Maggie bowed her head demurely. Anything to break the spell he had over her.

Then he kissed her palm. The air nearly crackled between them, and she wondered if anyone else noticed or could tell.

"It matters not," he said.

"What?"

"Anything but you and I, today."

He kept hold of her hand and introduced her to his closest and oldest friends. They were respectful and gentlemanly, as was Greylen. But she knew from experience these men were all warm and friendly one minute, kings of their castle the next.

She noticed the priest speaking with Gwen and went to introduce herself. She'd always found comfort in men of the cloth and knew she would here, too. There was warmth in the priest's eyes.

"Father Michael, I've heard only the nicest things about you. I'm so pleased to make your acquaintance."

"Ah, Lady Margaret."

"'Tis just plain Maggie, father."

"Well, then just plain Maggie," he said cheerily. "I'm pleased to meet you as well."

"Are you sure you have time for this today? You must be very busy."

The man looked at her sympathetically. "'Tis nigh on tradition here at Seagrave to preform nuptials... opportunely."

Everyone around snickered. Maggie was proud of herself though, when instead of snapping, like she wanted to, she let it roll right off her.

"I can hear you." She told them in a singsong voice.

Out of the corner of her eye, she saw Callum signal Father Michael. The priest cleared his throat and said, "Why don't we begin?"

The air felt thick as they gathered before him. Gwen stood to her left, Callum to her right, with Grey beside him. Lady Madelyn made a move to stand, and Maggie turned to her. "Please, no." The last thing she wanted was for that poor, dear woman to have to stand through a ceremony. Dar and Ronan took her cue and stood sentinel on either side of her chair.

It turned out to be a nice intimate arrangement. She and Callum were surrounded by people who truly cared about Callum, and by extension, her.

For a moment she pictured her own mother, and Celeste, and all the others who she wished could be by her side, and felt her eyes flood with tears. Callum's face swam before her and a moment later, as Father Michael's voice buzzed in her ear, Callum reached out and cupped her face, gently brushing her tears away.

It was terribly thoughtful, and she was struck once again by how he handled himself. He didn't draw undue attention to the situation, merely stepped in to do what needed to be done.

He stood as her rock, and she decided right then and there, that although she would steel herself from further heartache, while here she would honor and support him from this day forward.

How fitting on the end of that thought, she'd heard the question that would seal her fate in this century.

"I will." She said clearly, never wavering her gaze from him.

"The ring." The priest said, and Maggie inhaled sharply. It was all becoming so real.

Callum reached into his pocket and in the palm of his hand lay two delicate interlocked bands. Her heart caught in her throat for a brief moment when she realized this must have been what had drawn him to the smithy's incredibly early this morning.

When he slipped it onto her finger, it fit so perfectly Maggie gasped. Like everything since she fixed the jewel in the sword.

Could Callum and Dunhill—and the fifteenth century—really be her destiny?

CHAPTER TWENTY-FOUR

Callum fingered the bands, now in place on Maggie's hand. The idea came to him last night of joining two together. Its significance was twofold. To bear homage to this solemn second union they were both entering into; and they should be bound with no beginning, no end. As he looked into her eyes, 'twas exactly how he felt.

Bound to her.

Not only because of the way they were physically pulled to one another, but because he knew something deeper was at play. Callum cared not to question it further.

He knew it as sure as he knew he needed air to breathe, Maggie of Sinclair—O'Roarke was his touchstone.

His salvation.

He wished for their unity to last through eternity.

Let it be so.

He breathed those words, and she tilted her head ever so slightly as if she'd heard them. He watched her, while the priest's words sounded for what felt like perpetuity. She was a vision to behold.

When she'd walked into the room with Gwen, he'd noticed something in her bearing had changed in the hours since he'd last seen her. He wasn't quite sure what, but there was a difference. He watched her carry herself as regally as any noble he'd ever seen. And he'd seen his fair share.

Her deep wine-colored dress with shocks of black looked stunning against her skin, reminding him of what she'd felt like earlier, pressed to his body with only her thin chemise betwixt them. He'd merely meant to kiss her, a bit soundly perhaps, but when she'd met him move for move, he'd taken things to another level.

Callum staved off the deep rumble emanating from low in his throat such recollections evoked, and focused on her pretty eyes, a bit darker while her lips shined a glossy rose. He'd taken much liberty when she'd followed him into his chamber. He'd meant what he'd said, though. No offence was taken to her words.

Concerned for her welfare when he heard her cry. The sound pierced him deeply, and he would have done anything to soothe her. 'Twas just that as he stood in the threshold of her room, filled with servants and fluffery, he'd realized he'd walked in on her preparations.

Preparations for their nuptials.

He'd never expected her to follow him to his room and was shocked to find her in front of him when he'd sat to remove his boots. The way her robe had parted without her notice as she'd removed them was something to behold. The lighting just so.

While she offered an explanation, he had a lovely view of her. When she'd lifted his chin, all he could think of was making her his. Callum had been desperate to open it fully, but had resisted—even congratulated himself on the resistance—until she responded to his kiss with more intensity than he'd ever expected. He'd never entertained anything of the such before.

Callum held her at nights, in her bed when she cried out, but he'd been content merely at the feel of her in his arms. And of the times he'd kissed her, only twice afore that morning, he was simply enjoying the natural course of how this attraction between them deepened. Bedding her was not, and until this morn, had not been heralded in his mind.

Now that changed.

He'd thrown that gauntlet of sharing her bed this eve in the course of their earlier banter. However, he'd every intention to woo her until she was ready. Callum was confident it would not be long before their union was fully consummated.

Father Michael droned on, and Callum knew he should pay more attention, but the words mattered little. He finally heard the blessed question at hand, and answered, "I will."

When he kissed his bride, he did so meaningfully, but chastely. Since everyone present knew the reason for their union, there were no boisterous shouts of glad tidings, though the sentiment prevailed. There would be no ribbing of any sort, whether in reference to bedding or plain crass revelry.

Cook prepared a luncheon and aside from one silent toast, out of deference to Maggie's feelings, when they all raised a glass together, they dined as they would for any other meal.

When they stood from the table, again Maggie bowed her head demurely to him and curtsied to all present. He'd looked to Gwen, at a loss to her somewhat detached behavior, but Gwen merely shrugged.

"We have much to do today." He said, taking a lock of her hair and moving it behind her shoulders. In truth, he wanted to touch her.

"We?" She asked, looking at him for what seemed like the first in some time.

Callum had the odd sensation, now that they were married, there was a hollow betwixt them. He missed their closeness of only days ago.

When he motioned to the men behind him, she said. "I'll see you at supper, then?"

"This afternoon," he corrected her. "We've a game in the courtyard. Come watch."

"Of course," she said. Though there was no light in her eyes.

They'd gone their separate ways, and he spent the next few hours with Grey, Dar, and Ronan. When they returned to the keep, Gwen was in the Great Hall with her little ones.

"Maggie?" He asked.

"She fell asleep in the solarium. I don't think she slept much last night."

He understood. It had been late when she cried out and he'd been restless himself. Callum left Maggie undisturbed and changed, then instructed Anna to rouse his wife in an hour or so... he tripped over his words a moment, when he'd said them... *His wife.*

The enormity once again took him unawares.

He'd kept a watchful eye for her throughout the game. Which, he had to admit, was quite enjoyable. When Maggie stepped through the keep's main doors, warm beverage in hand, whatever sip she'd taken spewed forth.

Callum laughed heartily and looked to Gwen, who beamed that she'd called it correctly. Rubbing her fingers and thumb together, telling those involved in the wager to pay up.

"What in God's name is going on here?" Maggie cried incredulously.

"'Tis foot-ball!" He claimed exuberantly. "Gwen taught us."

She gave Gwen a horrified look. "Gwen you can't keep messing with things. Coffee is one thing, well, and quiche, and zip sauce, and God knows whatever else you've introduced around here. *And*, I admit it, okay—selfishly, I'm thrilled you've brought these things to Scotland a little ahead of the curve. But football? American football? What were you thinking?"

Gwen smiled. "Have no worries, Maggie. We have a saying around here, remember."

"Good Lord... What happens at Seagrave—"

"Stays at Seagrave!" Called the courtyard.

If for no other reason than to touch her again, Callum came up the steps, plucked the drink from her hand and took a sip. Then he gathered her close and kissed the side of her face. Forcing himself to live in the moment and push aside his earlier worries, something had changed betwixt them. When he felt her embrace him back and lean her head into his kiss, he let himself relax, too. Gladdened, he set her upon her feet and joined the crowd awaiting his return.

They wrapped up their game with the children a short time later. Then the real fun began, as only the men remained on the field. It was a rousing sport and one they took seriously. Gwen yelled a few times to "tone it down," but they ignored her.

A bit sore and a knock to his forehead later, Callum followed the others up the stairs to clean up for supper. Maggie held his hair back, eyeing his wound.

"Do you have something for this, Gwen?" She asked.

Callum bit back a smile. If she could care for his minor cut, she might care for him more deeply, too.

"Aye. I'll send it to your chamber." Gwen told her before turning to him with instructions to wash the abrasion thoroughly before Maggie put anything on it. He left Maggie outside her chamber and went to take a much needed bath.

When she exited her room sometime later, he was waiting on the bench, as had become their custom while at Seagrave. Her hands brushed through his hair as she stood before him and she dabbed some of the ointment onto his scrape, giving him a soft smile.

Dinner was livelier than lunch, praise be, and much of the talk centered around tomorrow's festival. Gavin and Isabelle's absence and Aidan's later than usual arrival.

KIM SAKWA

They played a game of cards afterward, prompting Maggie's only outburst of the night. "Poker, Gwen! Really!"

He winked at her while they all laughed. When she joined in with the revelry, Callum laughed even harder.

It was a cutthroat game. Each one of them was competitive. Countless hands later, they excused themselves and Callum walked her upstairs, more eager with every step.

"Callum," she said, sounding slightly nervous. "*Are you sharing my bed tonight? I seem to remember you making such a declaration earlier.*"

"I would be satisfied if only to hold you," he told her, meaning it.

She seemed placated by his words and did not demur. "If you may allow me some time," she said. Then, as if reading his confusion about how much time and for what, she clarified, "Mayhap half an hour or so?"

He inclined his head, and realized they'd fallen into this odd, polite, and silent communication. With luck, such formalities would be gone soon.

A short time later, Callum found her chamber door open, and when he entered, she was sitting before her vanity, brushing her hair. She offered a small smile in the reflection of the mirror.

He saw to the fire, then went to her, holding out his hand. She looked up and hesitated.

"I would but hold you, Maggie." He repeated, hoping to reassure her. "Let's dispel this awkwardness, please. We should feel closer, not further apart."

"I'm sorry, you're right."

He should be pleased with her acknowledgement, but she looked down as she said it. He knelt before her. "Maggie, is it more?" When she shook her head, he lifted her chin. "Then please look at me. I would see your face and your pretty eyes."

She lay her hands on his shoulders and shrugged. "I suppose I'm acting childish, or more nervous than I should. I swear, I'm trying to do nothing of the sort. In my defense, I've never been married before."

"How lucky for me that I am the one who calls you wife."

An odd look crossed her features, and he had a feeling he'd struck a nerve. Suddenly the room might be more crowded. Some things he realized could not be avoided, and though pitfalls may await them unknowingly, they need move through and forward, regardless.

"Come, I'll show you how we do this at night. Allow me to hold you. We can talk, mayhap even laugh, like we have before."

She'd begun to play with his hair, he was sure absently. Though Maggie had projected a tempered front the entire day, her actions gave her away. He loved the feel of her fingers skimming about his neck, and let them linger there a moment before he reached for her hands and stood, walking her to the bed. The covers had been turned down, and he foisted her up and onto the center.

Maggie chuckled, and the sound warmed his heart. He followed her down, stretching and getting comfortable before laying on his side, and turning her so her back pressed to his front. Mayhap she would feel better like this.

They were quiet for a few minutes. In all honesty, he was more contented than he could remember.

Then she began moving and adjusting her position.

"Maggie, if you wish to remain chaste, cease wiggling your bottom."

She giggled.

God's bones.

He leaned back and turned her so she lay on her back. "Maggie of Si—O'Roarke." He smiled down at her. "I don't think I can recall ever hearing such a sound from your lips."

She laughed again, accompanied by an adorable snort this time.

He laughed aloud himself. Unbidden by the lightness of the moment, he kissed her affectionately, a mere peck as it were.

The interlude did much to dispel the quiet and underlying tension. They stayed there, he just above her and she looking up at him.

When she laid her hand against his chest, he thought perhaps he'd gone too far and started to pull away.

"No." She shook her head. "I just want to touch you." She placed her hand back to where it was, firmly this time. He remained still, his breaths shallow, as he awaited her indication.

She spent a considerable amount of time just touching him, brushing her hand back and forth across his chest. Her eyes narrowed in contemplation.

After a long moment, she met his gaze. "Maybe we should get this over with."

If he wasn't worried about upsetting her, he would have thrown his head back and laughed. Instead, he smiled unable to help it, and chuckled a little. He took the hand she had upon his chest and brought it to his lips, kissing her palm.

"I can assure you, Maggie, *this* is nothing to get over with."

"You know what I mean," she said, rolling her eyes.

"I should take great offence to—" Mirth bubbled from inside and he laughed. "What *you* imply, and my thoughts of *this* are obviously very different."

She laughed and swatted his chest, and not a second later he fell into one of those fits of laughter he couldn't stop. He nigh on cried, it was so humorous. She laughed too, and he wondered a moment if mayhap Grey was right. Women from the future *were* daft. It couldn't just be Gwen and Maggie.

Then he laughed all the more.

Whatever the case, it seemed this spell of good cheer, regardless the cause, was just what they'd needed. Any remaining tension, now seemed gone.

"But seriously." She said once they'd stopped.

"But *seriously*," he repeated, teasing her funny way of talking. He knew, too, it was important to make sure they were thinking one and the same thing, and explained. "If I had planned to bed you—and just so we're clear on the *this* of this. Had I planned to bask in your glory tonight. In your beauty." He kissed the side of her face. "Your warmth."

He kissed the other side. "And your body." He swept his fingers through her hair, arranging it across the pillow, just so, before continuing. "If I planned on enjoying my good fortune in having you as my wife, by the consummation of our marriage, symbolized as I fill you completely. Making you only mine from this day forward. I would have but started before the fireplace.

I would have kissed you, Maggie, until you clung to me like you had this morning. When the scent of your arousal filled the air. God help me 'twas enough to make me almost lose myself then and there. All I wanted to do was to reach down and touch you. To feel your wetness and pet you till you nigh on purred for me.

I would have brought you to the brink of ecstasy, merely to do so again, and again, until I'd no choice than to thrust myself deep inside of you. God's bones I imagine it now and I swear I can feel it."

Her eyes glazed over, and he knew he'd stirred her. It wasn't his intention, when he'd first began his explanation, but now it was too late.

"Can you feel it too, Maggie?"

Throughout all of this, she had simply stared at him, expressionless. He knew not her reaction, so he leaned in and kissed her. Testing her response, ready to pull back again if necessary.

"Take you shirt off, Callum. Please," she said, breathing against his lips.

It was discarded in a blink. Before he knew how it happened, they were kissing and clutching at each other in a frenzy.

He tried to slow them down. "Maggie..."

"Callum, you're my husband, right?" She asked, her gaze fixed on his intensely.

"Aye."

"I can tell you anything, right?"

Her question splashed like a bucket of water over his head. He pulled back to look at her so she knew she had his full attention.

Callum braced himself, wondering what she must find of import just now. "You may tell me anything, Maggie. I will honor and protect you always."

"Callum," she clutched the sides of his head. "You have me so turned on, my body is screaming to be touched." The desperation of her cry and the look in her eyes so heady he stopped breathing for a second, and swelled to near bursting once again.

"It's like," her shallow breaths added to the already raw desire betwixt them. "My nerve endings *everywhere* are tight and raw and buzzing. Like," she brushed her fingers in fast order back and forth across his scalp to demonstrate. "Like that. Does that make sense? I've never felt so... So, on edge. Help me."

He couldn't believe his good fortune that she would express herself so openly, with both touch and words. Gone was the idea of a leisurely night of slow and easy pleasure.

He certainly would not say he was disappointed.

"Allow me to be of service," he breathed. Capturing her lips in a searing kiss, pulling her tight against him. She moaned as they fed off each other. He was stunned by the level of passion he felt betwixt them.

He couldn't get enough of her.

Any of her.

He felt nigh on desperate as he suckled and nipped on her lips before plundering her with his tongue as their mouths found a perfect cadence. He couldn't seem to press her close enough to his body and realized she must feel the same as they clutched and clung to one another.

'Twas the most passion he'd ever felt. God's bones, she had him on the edge already and they'd only just begun.

He sat up, taking her with him. Without a word, she lifted her arms and wriggled her body as he pulled the chemise from her. Groaning at the sight of her naked form, he reached out to skim the back of his hand across her fair skin and swell of her breasts. Callum would have spent more time looking at her lovely features and touching her reverently, but Maggie was in no mood for slow explorations.

He would retread such territory later.

In truth, they had all the time in the world. The thought excited him even further. For now, he went about the business of pleasing his wife.

Her naked body pressed against his was a satisfaction of its own. Her smooth skin *everywhere* was a wonder he delighted in. They soon became lost again in heady, carnal kisses. Grateful his britches provided a modicum of restraint, so this moment might last until he at least saw her sated. He slipped her leg over his waist and cupped her bottom, with the intent of getting her into a better position to touch her... discover her... please her.

Yet he groaned and fit her warmth snuggly against his erection, their hips rocking in an excruciating blissful rhythm.

He broke their kiss as he untangled their bodies and sat up, thinking his heart might burst from his chest. "God's bones, Margaret. I feel like an undisciplined lad."

"*Call-um*," she was trying to pull him back.

"Nae, my heart." He brushed his fingers through his hair, scratching his scalp in hopes of getting a hold of himself. Then he laid back down next to her, stuffing a pillow betwixt them.

She chuckled.

He had to admit it *was* humorous.

In all his life he'd never had this problem, this feeling of being so frenzied. He'd had his fair share of passion until... well, until. "Grant your husband a boon."

She smiled knowingly, her cheeks a warm rosy glow, eyes still glazed by desire. Aye, they were both caught up in this... this madness. Then she ran her fingers down the side of his face. "Kiss me again, Callum. Please. I can't seem to get close enough to you."

He knew exactly how she felt and pulled her in tight again. His control returned, with much help of the thick down barrier of the pillow. He spent long minutes kissing her again, stroking her from her fingertips to her navel. Gently touching her breasts and cupping each with his hand. He rolled her nipples, small tight buds, applying a bit of pressure to gauge her sensitivity.

Her verbal cues were most helpful.

His wife was not quiet in bed.

He pressed a bit harder, and her gasp of pleasure followed by a heady moan went straight to his groin.

While he still kissed her, he caressed her legs, spreading them wide, but did not touch her. Building her anticipation, he went back to her breasts for only a moment. Kneading and rolling and pinching before finally sweeping the back of his hand down the center of her chest, across her navel, and stopped atop her mound, a silky and smooth swath of skin.

Then he skimmed her center, pressing his hand against her. His fingers slipped easily between her folds—his wife drenched from their foreplay. And as he slowly brought his fingers up, applying just enough pressure, she moaned and gasped as he found her pleasure point.

"*Caaalluuum.*"

God's bones.

He circled her steadily, no teasing, no drawing it out further. Callum felt her body's first twitch, then felt her muscles tense. He held his breath, riding to the crescendo with her. Then his sweet Maggie burst as her body was engulfed in vibration.

He kissed her and continued to pet her while she calmed. Then tossed the pillow aside and shucked his britches so fast he nigh on ripped them.

She motioned with her hands and whispered, "Callum. Please. I want you inside me."

He settled on top of her, and she tilted her hips, reaching between them wrapping her hand around him. Yet he couldn't seem to get far. She started to get frustrated, mayhap panicked.

"Nae," he gave her a smile and shook his head. "Shh. 'Tis fine, love."

He felt like he had not a care in the world. Maggie was his, and he was about to have her. In full. A mere bit of positioning was all that was needed. He grabbed the pillow again and pushed it beneath her bottom, tilting her just so. Then clasped her hands. "Ready?"

She nodded and looked on the verge of tears. "Maggie? Is it something else? Am I hurting you?"

"Nae, Callum. Please. I would have you feel this, this whatever it is that is consuming me. I still feel strung so tight."

Ah, that he understood.

She nodded, waiting. With that, he tilted his hips back before thrusting himself completely inside. His head nearly exploded in pleasure and he would swear his eyes shed a tear or two.

'Twas the most incredible experience he'd ever had.

All thirty seconds of it before he released with his wife's name on his lips.

CHAPTER TWENTY-FIVE

Maggie awoke in Callum's arms, her cheek pressed to his chest. Their limbs tangled together like a game of twister gone mad. When she stirred, he kissed the top of her head and sighed contentedly, which was exerting more energy than she could manage at the moment.

Impressive. She chuckled to herself, and settled back against him. They lay that way for what could have been minutes or hours, watching the early light slowly creep into the room.

After some time, Callum lifted her until they were eye to eye, a slow, knowing grin spreading across his face. One Maggie felt herself mimicking. It would be ridiculous if it weren't so perfect. Pulling her closer to him, Callum brushed his lips over hers, nudging her affectionally, poignantly. Then he smiled and wrapped her in his long, powerful arms.

Maggie heard him attempt to say *something*, felt it rumble against her own chest, but it came out as a croak. She smiled and reached over him to grab the cup of water from the nightstand.

One of many they'd shared throughout the night. The last, after she insisted they change the bed sheets. At the time he still had his voice, and his "Ah" in thinking she had a brilliant idea was well appreciated. That, and the fact he helped her remake the bed. Not that he needed extra points but come on, he helped her make the bed.

They'd also taken great care in cleaning up.

Each other.

Twice.

Who knew a sponge bath could be so erotic and satisfying?

Sated, she'd crawled across the bed, well into the middle of the night. Callum followed her back on the fresh, cool linens. He'd pulled her against him, arranged the covers around them, tucked her head beneath his chin, and she'd fallen asleep almost instantly.

He looked at her now as he took a sip, reaching out to stroke the side of her face. "Ah," he mustered. "I have sound."

Maggie grinned again from ear to ear, still on a post-coitus high. She'd never imagined a night so perfect. Who knew off-the-chain-hot and sweetly endearing melded so well together in one man?

They *so* did.

She'd never been more turned on in her life.

Never.

Callum knew just what to say and how to say it. How to affect her with merely a look. Which was something Maggie hadn't known was possible.

He found every pleasure point on her body. And by the look on his face, he was quite pleased about it. More than once he had her wound so tight without even touching her, she'd begged before he grinned mischievously and relented.

This chemistry between them was unearthly.

She was desperate to know if he felt it too. To Maggie, it was as if the insides of her body were spinning a hundred miles an hour. She'd tried to explain it, show him even. Her eagerness is what had elicited him giving her all of his attention, and his intense focus on her drove her crazier.

He seemed very pleased about that, too.

And then it was everything else besides the hot stuff. He was sweet and genuine. She loved that he could go from being so in control to showing her just how out of control she made him.

Images from the night before continued to pass through her mind as they shared a few slow, lazy kisses. This seemed to be all either could manage. Both tapped out by their night of passion.

When it became too bright in the room to ignore, they dressed and walked hand in hand into the kitchen, keeping as close to one another as possible, rubbing against each other just because they could

Glancing out the large picture window on the stairs, Maggie allowed her mind to wander to the day ahead. Callum and Grey planned to see to the labor-intensive festival preparations, which meant she would be spending more time with Gwen. Maggie welcomed it.

They'd become close in the short time she'd been at Seagrave, practically attached at the hip since day one.

Maggie liked that Gwen would seek her out, knocking on her door to invite her on her latest errand or have her taste something new Cook whipped up.

Maggie loved watching Gwen run the inside of the castle. Frankly, in awe of how a twenty-first century woman made a real home for herself here in the 1400's. She was blissfully happy, even without any modern comforts. That clearly was due to Greylen—Gwen constantly interrupted him and his men with something silly, eager to see her husband during their busy days.

Maggie realized with a pang she missed that, checking in with that special someone, and squeezed Callum's hand.

The kitchen in sight at the end of the hall. She let herself imagine what her life might be like.

Here.

With Callum.

A real, permanent life. Not one where her time here was temporary. Or where she still held on to a hope she'd be whisked back to her own time. Could she make *this* her own time? There was a living example right in front of her. One filled with joy and promise.

Gwen and Grey were already sitting at the table, children in hand. If Maggie hadn't wanted coffee and breakfast so badly, she would have avoided Gwen for at least a week to save herself from her new friend's gloating.

Maggie could only imagine what she looked like, loopy and loose next to Callum. She definitely had "just had sex" hair. Hopefully, the neon sign on her forehead would stop flashing soon.

Gwen and Greylen each raised a brow when they entered, making Callum chuckle. Maggie, bit her lip and said nothing.

Callum pulled out a chair for her then took the seat next to it. When Maggie sat, Callum did, too, and dragged her closer. His hand was on her thigh. Even though he wasn't doing anything with it but resting it there, it was causing her fits. His large, heavy hand.

There.

Well, it was almost too much. Her stomach whirled all over again. She hadn't even had any coffee yet.

Surely, the intensity of their physical attraction would wear off soon. Maggie wasn't sure how she'd get through each day otherwise.

For a long few moments, no one said anything.

ANYTHING.

Finally, Gwen broke. "Well, this is awkward." She said, clearly suppressing a grin.

After another moment of silence, Grey said, "Good God, they're speechless."

Callum gave them both a feigned withering look, but said, "Morning." As he poured Maggie a cup of coffee. Or, at least he tried to say "Morning." His voice was still on the raspy side. As he poured his own cup, his cheeks flamed red, and so did hers.

They all laughed then, the tension finally broken.

Maggie caught Gwen's eye and was greeted with her *I-told-you-so* look.

Rolling her eyes, Maggie threw her napkin at Gwen in mock annoyance and grabbed one of Cook's buttery rolls from the pretty basket in the middle of the table. As she took a bite, the yeasty dough melted in her mouth. She tore off a large piece and put it on Callum's plate, just as he was in the process of halving a piece of quiche to place on hers.

"Good God," Greylen said. "Look at them? I don't think I can sit through this."

Gwen laughed then and threw a roll across the table, which Callum caught with a wink. It did the trick to dispel the remaining awkwardness. Soon conversation turned to the business of the day, with the final preparations of the festival.

Listening to the chatter around the table, it surprised Maggie to realize how *normal* it all felt. Despite that this marriage hadn't come about in the normal way—well, okay, this *was* the normal way for the century she was living in now. *What was it Father Michael had said*? Ah, right. Weddings at Seagrave were opportune. Indeed.

It didn't matter, normal or not normal. Although she and Callum had to get married because of the circumstances, it still felt right. That was what was so weird about it. It *felt* so right, Maggie was beginning to have doubts about steeling her heart from him. A plan that seemed so sound— *essential*—to maintaining some kind of agency and freedom, felt almost silly.

In fact, she felt more in control today, more secure, frankly in everything, than she had since the day she'd put that jewel in the sword and landed outside the Abbey. Something had happened last night. Not merely sex, either. Last night *was* intense, but it was the intimacies they'd shared in between. That they had been sharing over the preceding months. Their connection in bed felt parallel to how their friendship had grown and deepened, slowly and indelibly.

It was the bond they'd forged in friendship these past months that meant the most to Maggie, even still. If they hadn't become so close otherwise, she wasn't certain they'd have been as comfortable with each other last night.

It lent itself to deepening this closeness they had with each other. She did love Callum, it just wasn't that silly 'shout from the rooftops', showy, 'I can't get enough of you' love. There was no girlish need to gush how much she loved him. Her feelings weren't those kinds of feelings. Or so she told herself.

Watching him now, talking to Grey about horses of all things, Maggie felt a warmth in her chest, a deep respect and admiration for him. She liked him as a human being. Callum was a good man. Honest, intriguing, and intelligent, and even those new facets of him she'd never seen before. The implacable warrior who... who made her feel like in his kingdom, she was his queen. And as such, no harm would befall her.

She knew now when they'd first arrived at Seagrave and he'd gone all Tarzan on her; it wasn't for show. He *was* marking her for all to see. Claimed in a custom as old as time. At least in these times as was the custom she supposed.

Being claimed by Callum wasn't anything negative. He was a very loving man—even before last night. She felt safe with him. She had every intention of honoring and supporting Callum in everything he did. He was deserving of both. And she would make sure he knew it.

The physical stuff, well, that was a perk.

As she watched Gwen and Greylen tend to their children, the love between them was clear. Maggie marveled again at how completely happy Gwen really was here. That she considered not just Seagrave, but the fifteenth century her forever home.

Maggie envied that about her. She still missed Celeste, her old job, pizza delivery, and modern plumbing. Maggie wondered yet again, if the sensation of belonging would come for her, too. She still fantasized, though much less than she used to, about the sword coming to life, and beckoning her home. But she realized, even if she *was* here forever, it might be okay.

Like one hundred percent okay, living *here* in the fifteenth century with Callum.

She had a friend now in Gwen. A friend who could understand exactly what she was going through and where she was coming from. Literally. Maggie was surprised to realize if she was given the choice now—stay here or go home—she wasn't sure what she'd choose. For now, being Callum's wife was not a hardship. Hopefully the rest, as they say, would work itself out.

After breakfast, the plan was for a bit of divide and conquer to prepare for the festival. Callum, Grey and the other men would see to the set up outdoors and in the Great Hall. While Maggie would join Gwen in any last-minute details of décor and menu prep.

As they traipsed from one end of the castle to the other, Gwen filled her in, that until two years ago, the autumn festival had always been at Dunhill. That surprised

Maggie—Dunhill wasn't exactly the bustling metropolis Seagrave felt like.

Still, Maggie reasoned, it made sense that after Fiona had passed away, and Callum had taken up residence at Seagrave, they'd moved it here. According to Gwen, the first festival had been ten years ago, and started out as just a bonfire by the water as the five men, Greylen, Callum, Dar, Aidan, and Ronan paid tribute to Allister and Fergus for bringing them together. For educating, training, and molding them into the men they would become. Over the years it slowly grew, and they decided to make a special night of it for everyone on the property, though the men kept their tribute private amongst themselves.

Even though this year's was to be the largest festival yet, Gwen had everything under control. Or so it seemed. The woman was a whirlwind and had everyone at Seagrave wrapped around her finger, her husband included.

When everything was as ready as it would ever be, Gwen and Maggie went their separate ways to get dressed. Nessa and Rose made her a beautiful burgundy linen dress to be worn over a long-sleeved, soft beige chemise. Maggie admired how the slim, fit bodice of the tunic and the corset, emphasized her breasts and waist. The slightly wider skirt had gusset drapes with soft pleats and the entire dress was trimmed with a thick embroidered band. Lastly, she tied a wide choker around her neck. It was really stunning in a medieval bad ass kind of way.

While she dressed, Maggie realized she hadn't seen Callum all day. She was further surprised by how much it hurt her feelings to find he wasn't waiting on the bench in the hall. Thrown by what felt like a slight and how deeply it affected her, Maggie sensed her spirits sinking, despite knowing she was about to spend all evening with him.

If a small disappointment sent her spinning, maybe she would have to rethink her earlier feelings, and go back to compartmentalizing where Callum was concerned.

Maybe she wasn't ready. Maggie had bared herself to him, trusted him emotionally and physically, and now a little thing like not meeting her outside her door made her feel abandoned. He likely had a good reason.

Even so, this had been a good lesson in guarding her heart.

As she made her way downstairs, she stopped to stare out of the large picture window on the landing. It was a place she'd found herself lingering on more than one occasion, and based on the many others she'd witnessed do the same, Maggie figured it was a favorite spot of everyone who lived here.

She pressed her hand to the glass, lost a bit in her reflection. Her sense of belonging in this century clearly more tenuous than she'd realized. A wave of homesickness washed over her and Maggie braced herself for an evening of revelry she wasn't sure she felt up to anymore.

There was nothing worse than feeling alone while surrounded by tons of people. Even the wedding band around her finger, that only yesterday made her heart melt, didn't feel all that special anymore. Now that Callum had gotten what he wanted—her belonging to him—had he stopped needing her so intensely?

She'd considered him one of the most thoughtful people she knew, but that appeared to be slipping. She had felt so close to him this morning. But it all seemed a bit empty now. The last week had been a roller coaster of emotions, one she was clearly still on, and at a low point she hoped wasn't the end of it. It seemed impossible they'd left Dunhill only six days ago.

So much had changed.

With dusk upon them, the glow of bonfires was visible from the shore below. Maggie watched as a few riders made their way down the steep path. In the courtyard, tables and chairs were set up for the feast Cook and her staff had been preparing for days. For those who couldn't take the chill of the outdoors, the Great Hall would provide a warm, inviting place.

Maggie saw Callum now, standing with his friends in the courtyard, looking handsome as always. Tonight, he was wearing his standard breeches, boots, and shirt, but he had a heavier dark sleeveless piece over it.

She'd met Aidan, the last of their brotherhood, when he'd arrived earlier and found her and Gwen in the kitchen. He'd seemed kind, congratulating her on her nuptials and apologized for missing the occasion. Maggie envied the connection these men had, even though they only came together as a group once a year.

Down below, Callum smiled at something one of the men was saying. She supposed she was happy for him. He was enjoying himself.

She just wasn't in the mood anymore.

Before she turned, she saw Greylen lift Gwen atop his horse and climb up behind, hugging her before kissing the side of her face. She reached back and wrapped her arms around his neck. Maggie loved watching them. Their love was so obvious. It was astounding what an incredible life they had here together.

Only this morning, she wondered if she and Callum could be that happy one day.

CHAPTER TWENTY-SIX

Callum looked up as Maggie stepped back from the window. He'd kept watch on her figure there for the last few minutes, eager for her to join him. When he realized she was lingering, he knew something was amiss.

Wondering what had upset her, he left the company of his brethren and headed back to the keep. Thinking he would have found her on her way out as he was on his way in, he spent a minute or two wandering the crowded hall. Finally, with no sight of her, he took the stairs.

He'd been anticipating being in her company since they'd parted this morning. Given what had transpired *as* they parted, he'd assumed she had been eager to see him, too.

After breakfast he'd walked her back to her room, pressed her against the door he'd closed and kissed her like he wanted to do all the time lately. He'd pulled back to look at her, and she'd nodded. They'd both grinned.

Callum was ready to make good on one of the many declarations he'd made last night when he explained in detail the things he would do to her. Some of which he'd said he would do right here, with her pressed up against this very wall. Unfortunately, they'd been interrupted seconds later by an insistent rap on the door, and he whispered his promise to make good on it later.

Wondering what changed between then and now, Callum scanned the crowd from above on the landing. In case he'd somehow missed her. Not seeing his woman amongst them, he went straight to her room, thinking mayhap she'd forgotten something. There, he knocked lightly on her door, then opened it and called out her name.

The first wave of relief he felt upon seeing her, a vision in a dress Nessa and Rose had obviously taken great pains to make, was overtaken by dismay. Something was wrong with his Maggie, who was sitting on the bench at the end of the bed, looking forlorn. 'Twas not a sight that pleased him.

"Maggie?" He said again, softer this time.

She gave a tight smile and worried her hands in her lap. He walked up to her and lifted her chin.

"What's this?" He asked, brushing her cheek with his other hand.

She looked up between her lashes, and remarked half-heartedly. "Do we have to get into a whole debate about *this* again?"

He smiled softly at her attempt to make light of what troubled her, and sat beside her, taking her hand. "I thought you could tell me anything?"

"Are you going to kitchen-sink me about *everything* from last night?"

Her stab at levity missed the mark. "I'm willing to spend the entirety of the evening sorting this out, if need be. But please explain to me what kitchen-sink me means."

She threw him a small smile, and said, "It's when you throw something that happened back in someone's face."

He took offence at her illumination, but thought carefully about what she said. "Throwing or jesting?" He need be sure, to avoid doing so again. Maybe this was what Grey meant whenever he said twenty-first century women were all daft.

She shrugged. "Even if it's to tease, when it's at the other person's expense, it still hurts their feelings."

He took *their* to mean *her* and wondered what or who had hurt her feelings. 'Twas obvious she was highly sensitive. But first he'd apologize for his kitchen-sinking.

"I never meant to hurt your feelings. In all honesty, when I said *this*, I wasn't referring to our conversation last night. I should have started with—Margaret, what's bothering you *right now*?"

She gave him a sad look, then said. "I feel, small, and stupid, and silly now that you're here and being so nice—"

"First of all, they're feelings, Margaret. We all have them. They *all* have merit. Secondly, why wouldn't I be nice to you?" He hadn't meant to cut her off, but he needed to clear this up now. He was truly at a loss before he realized. "Wait, a moment. Is it *I* who hurt your feelings?"

"I thought you'd forgotten me." She shrugged. "I guess I felt left in the lurch."

The mere thought he'd forgotten about her was preposterous. Not that he would tell her so. He'd grown up in a household in essence run by two women, and had known Fiona to fall into rash moods, too. Especially when she'd been with child.

"I would never forget you. *Never*. Now, will you explain left in the lurch?" He'd a feeling and wasn't thrilled to be cast in such light.

She shrugged, "It means you... you abandoned me."

He jerked back in disbelief. *Stay calm, Callum.* He took a deep breath, but felt his voice rise when he spoke. "In truth? *This* is what you thought? That I'd abandoned you?"

She shook her head and placed her hand over his heart. "It's what I *felt*, Callum. My thoughts are a jumbled mess at the moment. It's been a whirlwind since we left Dunhill, wouldn't you say?"

"I would agree, Maggie. That said, I'm very happy to be in the place where we are now."

"I know. I'm not saying I'm not happy. I am... well, I was. It's just, when you weren't in the hall waiting for me," she covered her chest with her hand, and shook her head. "My heart constricted, and it scared me. Because I realized how much I've come to care for you and rely on you. And suddenly I was left feeling like you didn't care anymore."

At this, Callum softened and pulled her in slowly, grateful she did not resist. He held her a moment, pressing his lips to her forehead. He'd learned the importance and strategy of bringing one around to reason. In this case, a draw or surrender was the winning hand. He felt her relax as he rubbed her back.

"I'm going to presume you didn't receive my note?" He said, purposefully keeping his voice light.

She pulled back. "You left me a note?" There was a hopeful look on her face, a softening of her pretty eyes.

He smiled. God's bones. He loved this woman. Even upset, she'd spoken through her discomfort. He'd learned too, *no kitchen-sinking* from this day forward. Not even in jest.

"Margaret, do you truly believe I am so uncaring I would leave you for the entirety of the day? The day after we wed no less, and after we spent the most consequential night together?"

He kissed her then, as he'd wished to all day. As he wished to when he came inside to bathe and change and found she was still flittering about the keep with Gwen.

He'd been sorry he'd missed her. Bereft, actually. Like a lovesick lad he'd penned a note. "We are bound by God, by law, and bound by intimacy. Margaret, I lo—"

"No," she cried, and covered his mouth with her delicate hand. "No, don't say it." She shook her head.

"Why not?" He asked around her fingers.

She looked at him, clearly surprised he'd asked for an explanation. He'd have thought by now she would have realized he made informed decisions, when not acting on pure instinct. The more knowledge readily available, the better equipped he was to deal with whatever was at hand.

It took her a moment to answer. In truth, he wasn't entirely sure she was being honest with him, either.

"We are also bound by magic, or a spell, or whatever it is." She said, clearly choosing her words carefully. "And who knows how sound our foundation is. What if we're cursed to know love and loss, over and over again? For one, I'm not ready to tempt fate. Two, can we just be okay with the way things are now?"

"If that is your wish, aye." Her fear at hearing he loved her was quite real. He wasn't offended she didn't want the words.

They were mere words.

He would show her.

Callum would do everything in his power to make her as happy to be here, in this century, with him, as Gwen was to be with Grey. He had a ready example to emulate; he need only work to bring her the joy she rightly deserved.

He arranged her hair over her shoulders. "Let's find the note I penned, aye?"

She nodded, a small but genuine smile upon her lips. Hand in hand, they walked about her chamber. There, on the table before the fire, lay a tray of tea and biscuits.

Almost certain of what lay beneath, he gave his head a shake. Lo' and behold when he lifted said tray, it was right there for her to see. She grinned as he handed it to her, and he was so relived to show her he was not without thought or care. She broke the wax seal.

My dearest Margaret of O'Roarke, My Queen,

I anxiously await the hour... minute... and second until I have the pleasure of being in your company again. Look for me in the courtyard at the start of the festival.

Yours,
Callum Sebastian O'Roarke

"Well, I'm so glad we had this little talk." She beamed.

He laughed, knowing a full jest, and her poking fun at what transpired. "May I take you downstairs and hold you on my arm as we enjoy a night of revelry?"

She nodded and kissed him. An affectionate peck, but still, it thrilled him to no end. Then they left her chamber and, he hoped, her troubles behind.

He took her to the shore, riding with her in front of him on his stallion for the first time. Callum loved holding her thus as they made their way down the steep path. Then they walked from one end of the coastal inlet to the other. Six fires had been lit and roared still. He adjusted her cloak and wrapped his arm around her when he saw her shiver.

Noticing for the hundredth time the leather thong around her neck as he did so, he asked, "May I see your medallion?"

"You mean yours?"

"I believe it's precisely where it's meant to be." He told her as she reached up and untied it. "You know Gwen wears one too?" He chuckled, holding the familiar wolf in his hand. "At times she wears two."

"Really?"

"Aye." He brushed the side of her face tenderly. "Grey is the Mighty Dragon, Dar is the Fearless Griffin, Aidan is the Formidable Bear, and Ronan is the Imperial Hawk."

"And you're the little wolf?"

He laughed. "God's bones, Margaret—*Nae*!" 'Twas so humorous he nigh on cried again. "I *was* the little wolf as a child. I became the Proud Wolf as a man."

226

She rolled her eyes, muttering, "*Sor*-ry!" Callum couldn't help but laugh again.

Companionable silence fell between them then. Callum fingered the etching on the medallion once more, sobering as he looked to the sea and paid homage to his father. He took a deep breath before speaking again.

"Our fathers made each of us a medallion," he said, slowly holding up the one in his hand. "Each etched with our respective animals. One night, nigh on fifteen years ago, Fergus and Allister built a bonfire, much like this one, calling each of us of the brotherhood to gather there. They affixed the pieces around our necks, sliced into the palms of our hands, and made us take an oath. A blood oath to honor and protect those whom we bring into our care. To serve our people with integrity. Love with an open heart for all of our days. 'Tis a vow we commemorate yearly."

He pressed his lips to the wolf his father had carved for him, then re-affixed it around Maggie's neck. She shivered at his touch, then clasped his hand.

"Come, let's go drink, and dance, and be merry." He said, feeling very light all of a sudden.

"You dance?"

"I should take great offence, Margaret of O'Roarke. But I'll allow you to judge for yourself."

He grinned, leading her by the hand and pulling her in, mimicking the moves Gwen had taught Grey. At her astonished expression, he felt quite smug, and laughed, placing her hand around his neck, the other upon his chest.

Then commenced the night of revelry he'd never expected before Maggie of Sinclair O'Roarke walked into his life. They danced, they drank, they ate. It was one of the most memorable nights of his life.

She'd touched him repeatedly throughout the night, indicating, perhaps, she was more open than she realized. While she may think words meant all, in truth actions prevailed. Callum noted all the instances in which she sought his hand or wrapped her arm around his. She stroked the back of his neck whenever they were in one another's arms on the 'dance floor' as Gwen called it. They shared their drink, they shared their dinner.

God's bones.

If she only wished *not* to share the words I love you, he'd take it and still be the winner.

By the time they made it to her chamber, the light touches throughout the evening had driven them both into a frantic state. The moment the door closed behind them, Callum pressed her against the wall and kissed her deeply.

His hands found her breasts, and he fondled them while unlacing the front of her dress. Once freed, he bent to caress them with his cheek. His lips first suckling, then gently biting down on her hardened nipples until she gasped.

The sound shot right to his groin.

He turned her to face the wall and in one fluid movement, reached beneath her skirts to remove her stockings, then lifted her leg and bent it at the knee so she was pressed between the wall and his body, exposing her nicely for his ministrations.

"Are you okay, love?" He whispered, knowing her bared breasts lay against the cool stone wall.

She moaned "Yes, Callum. Please."

He caressed her bottom, and the backs of her thighs, teasing and taunting her. "Please what?" He breathed.

"Touch me."

Oh, he touched her. He swept his hand toward her from the side of her thigh, pressing against her heat and moisture. With her hooded pleasure point easily accessed from her position, he used his fingertips to pet her steadily, up and down. Applying just enough pressure, if she wanted more she need only push against him.

She moaned again and again. The heady combination of the sound and her scent making his chest nigh on burst once again. He helped her along, using his other hand to play with her entrance. Callum felt her tense and pressed a finger just inside as her tight muscles contracted repeatedly.

He fumbled with his britches, finally freeing himself enough to rub his erection in her heat. "*Callummm.*" She wiggled and tilted her hips against him.

"God's bone's Margaret," he rasped desperately, pressing himself inside.

She screeched as he filled her, and he stopped in fear he'd caused her pain.

"Maggie?"

"Oh, Callum. *Soooo* good, *soooo* deep."

He might not live to their first anniversary if his wife constantly kept him teetering at this height of excitement. Callum thrust again, and she nearly climbed up the wall on a gasp. He knew already she liked this position but thought mayhap they'd be more comfortable upon the bed.

At first, when he went to move them, she pouted, which he found provocative and enticing, so he promised to appease her in mere seconds. They helped each other undress and then she crawled upon the bed to lay so he might resume where they left off.

It was a beautiful sight as he came over her, taking great pains to arrange her hair across the linens just so. Then he lifted her hips and found purchase once more.

He was careful not to penetrate so deeply out of worry he'd hurt her. Even still, the pleasure was excruciating. It didn't help that Maggie ground herself against him making his effort of trying not to go so deep nigh on obsolete. He congratulated himself on the extended time he lasted inside her. Mayhap an extra minute or two, so he hoped.

He cleaned her afterwards, like he had the night before, gentle yet diligent. Then they slipped beneath the covers, and Maggie burrowed against his chest.

Callum held her as she slept, his mind alive with plans to make her happy.

He would see to it she never fretted over whatever magic had drawn them together by the bargain his mother made.

She was his, and he was hers.

There need not be more explanation.

CHAPTER TWENTY-SEVEN

Maggie's last day at Seagrave began with a start, waking alone to the feel of cool bed sheets. Her eyes shot open, and she breathed a sigh of relief at the sight of Callum standing by the window.

Aye, she was attached.

She watched him quietly, drinking in his form. This beautiful, proud man, her husband. This warrior from another century she'd married only days ago.

Already dressed, he stood tall and appeared to be deep in thought. He must have sensed her watching him because he turned to face her, his eyes intensely bright, and gave her the most delicious smile. His face was full of excitement and zeal at whatever he'd been devising, and it shone from his lips.

"Morning, love."

"Morning," she answered back, realizing this use of the word did not bother her. It felt more like an affectionate pet name than an intense declaration.

It wasn't that she didn't have deep feelings for him. *Duh*, of course she did. But she wasn't ready for the full pressure and weight of what *I love you* meant in this context. She had love for Callum, but she didn't know if she was capable of letting herself go any further.

There was truth to what she'd told him last night. She did wonder if this spell, or enchantment, or whatever, had a trap door. This was the real gist of it. What if she did give her heart to him, and then she had to go back? Or was given the chance? Would she take it? She wasn't entirely sure.

She felt she could be happy with Callum. But she didn't know whether it would be a full happiness. There was still this nagging something in the back of her mind. Something told her, it, *this* wasn't done.

She'd left Celeste.

Not on purpose. Still, she'd just... disappeared. If Maggie felt left in the lurch by Callum last night, how must Celeste feel? It was the one piece that still haunted her. The one she couldn't let go.

She watched now as he poured her a cup of coffee from the small tray on the secretary next to him, making her worry she'd missed breakfast.

"Did I sleep late?" She asked, accepting the cup from him and drinking deeply.

He shook his head. "Nae, I was up earlier than usual." He sat on the edge of the bed, and at once she felt his energy. He was practically vibrating with enthusiasm. She could almost see the gears turning in his head.

Maggie stretched and took another sip from her cup. It was nice to enjoy coffee in bed. But she had a feeling this display of vim and vigor of his meant he was ready to get on with the business of going home. To Dunhill. Then she saw the satchels on the bench at the end of her bed, and smiled wistfully. Her thoughts confirmed.

He shook his head. "Nae, no melancholy. We'll visit again. Come spring."

God, how she looked forward to that. Then suddenly wondered if she would still be here. Realizing she felt a pang of disappointment at the idea that she might not be, didn't help her confusion one bit.

How could she give herself to this man completely when she herself doubted her permanency here? It was something she had to get a grip on. She couldn't live half in and half out. Not now that they were married. It wasn't fair to either of them.

For now, she decided, she would be *in*, and give Callum what he deserved. A partner, a companion, and a lover who would support him in everything. She just wouldn't let herself fall too deep.

Maggie reached out to stroke his face, tracing his scar before moving her fingers through his hair and leaning forward to kiss him. She did love kissing this man. Especially like this, when there was no expectation of anything more. It was merely the intimacy of touch, that step beyond hand holding and hugging that solidified your togetherness as a couple.

"I promise we will return." He took her hand, fingering her band.

"I never said how much I love this band. It's beautiful and unique."

"I forged it with you and our union in mind," he told her.

So, he had made it. "I love it even more." She whispered, meeting his gaze.

"My oath to you is as solid and infinite as this ring, Margaret. That includes any promise I make to you, big or small. We'll see Seagrave again, with the first of spring."

She gave him a tight nod. Maggie believed him of course; it was just hard to leave Seagrave. Its liveliness, and the friendship she'd found with Gwen. Not to mention everything that had happened in this chamber. All she'd shared here with Callum.

Then, something struck her. Dunhill was to be her *home*. She would be the lady of the house. She started to bubble up with excitement, too. It would be nice to be back at Dunhill.

"Breakfast?" Callum asked, tearing Maggie from her thoughts. "When I went to get coffee, Cook was already preparing your favorites. I believe a trove of delights are being packed to get us home."

Hearing him say the word 'home' warmed her all over. She nodded. "Aye. Then I'll help you pack."

"My satchel's ready. I took the liberty to begin for you as well."

"You packed my things?" She asked, not sure if she should be appreciative or angry. "Like, you went through my stuff?"

"I folded your hanging dresses and put them atop some shoes, clearly not necessary for the journey home. Then placed them in your larger satchel," he explained. As if she were witless, and annoyed she questioned him.

"Thank you. I think."

"Why does that bother you?"

She'd struck a nerve and felt a bit bad. How could she have forgotten? *Callum need not be questioned.* Especially Liege Lord Callum. She supposed it was nice he did it. He was anxious to get home. It's not like she was hiding anything.

"I'm not sure it does. But what if there were things I had that were private?"

"*Ah,*" he said, realization dawning. "I did no poking about, Margaret. But... have you something to hide?"

"Well, I do possess *oddities,*" she reminded him with a lopsided grin.

He smiled, his face alight again. "Aye, you do." He kissed her. Another one of those just cover her lips, and pull ever so slightly. She really liked those. He titled his head then, obviously his mind not only on kissing her. "Oddities other than your jacks?"

She chuckled and nodded, not sure exactly how to explain what a cell phone was—unless, of course, he already knew about Gwen's. Maggie hoped the inhabitants here took their saying to heart.

If not, the world was going to be mightily changed by one Gwendolyn MacGreggor and her merry band of cohorts.

Maggie would have loved to linger over breakfast, but could tell Callum was already ten steps ahead and eager to be on their way. They would take a more roundabout route back, since they had a cart filled with supplies for the winter. And so, had to stick to roads wide enough to fit. This also meant their travel time to the cottage almost doubled.

She took a moment alone after breakfast to absorb all that happened over their stay at Seagrave. Gwen was upstairs with the baby. Callum and Greylen were outside, checking the wagon's sturdiness and inventorying the supplies they were taking back to Dunhill.

Standing in the grand foyer, Maggie turned slowly, committing to memory the feeling of being in this place, amongst these people. Sure, she'd be back, old hag magic permitting, but she knew it would never be like this. The first time.

So much happened here this past week. So much had changed. Her connection to Callum had grown so deep, and she'd made a new best friend. Coming here, had truly changed her life, yet again. She wanted to make sure this was one of those moments crystalized in her mind.

Never forgotten.

Maggie hugged Gwen goodbye, tearing up while they took one last look at each other. "I'll see you in the spring." Gwen said, nodding and wiping her eyes as Greylen put an arm around his wife. Maggie did the same, grateful for Callum's reassuring embrace as he led her to the cart and helped her up. She turned and waved one last time, sad to say goodbye to the MacGreggors and Seagrave.

By the time they stopped for lunch, Maggie felt a little better. Although, weird again for a different reason. It struck her she was sitting in a horse drawn cart, next to Callum, her husband, in the fifteenth century.

"You're about to enter another dimension..." Rang through her mind, from a really old show she'd streamed online. *Yeah, she was here.*

Shaking the odd feeling off, Maggie helped Callum with the horses, made a quick trip to the secluded brush, then set out the blanket Anna had packed for them. Callum grabbed the basket filled with Cook's treats, and stretched out on his side, laughing when she exclaimed, "Bird salad! Yum."

"Ha ha," He teased her. "It's chicken."

"Well, it's one of my favorites. Especially stuffed in these rolls."

They walked for a bit afterward, just to stretch their legs, then were off again. The sun setting when the cabin came into view.

Maggie marveled at the difference only a week made.

CHAPTER TWENTY-EIGHT

Callum saw to the horses while Maggie went inside to set up the dinner Cook had packed for them. That all taken care of, they ate at the small table in the tiny kitchen. His wife's pleasure at the meal caused him fits of laughter as she described what they were eating as yet another "reverse throwback."

"*But seriously*, Callum. See, this is a tenderloin medallion with hollandaise sauce."

"But *seriously*, Margaret, I'm about to take your portion and eat it myself."

Her expression changed to concern. "Oh, are you still hungry? Here, please. I can have it another time."

He'd only been teasing her, but one Margaret of O'Roarke showed her love and care. "I've had plenty," he told her. Then sat back to enjoy her sounds of delight as she ate.

After he helped her clean up, they sat by the fire, watching the flames dance as the burning wood crackled.

"Do you have music on your... What is it called? Your phone?" He asked as she lay between his legs, her back to his chest. He'd only heard a few pieces from Gwen's strange, and at first, startling device. After his initial shock, he found he rather enjoyed what she and Grey listened to.

She chuckled. "I do, but it's dead right now. It wasn't until I told Gwen I had it with me I even considered trying to charge it. I'll have to leave it out and see if it works."

"How so?" He asked, genuinely curious.

"My battery pack can run off energy collected from the sun."

"In truth?" He asked, wondering how it was possible.

"I think so. At least it used to." She said, shifting yet again.

"Turn over, and I'll rub your back and bottom."

She chuckled, "That's subtle."

He knew what she meant and laughed. "'Tis not what I had in mind." *Yet.* "I know you are sore. We had a long day sitting atop that wooden seat. No matter the cushioning, 'tis no easy feat."

He lasted much longer than he'd expected, considering his wife's moans of pleasure as he gently worked her tender spots. He made love to her by the fire afterward, the same spot only week ago he'd fought to keep her alive.

This time, instead of the frantic lovemaking they'd participated in up to now, their passions were long and languorous. Which held its own kind of force in its slow build. He held her long after she fell asleep, then carried her to bed, gathering her close once more, tucking her head beneath his chin.

It took some time for sleep to claim him, thinking of all that awaited back home. He'd spent hours talking to

Grey, Dar, Aidan, and Ronan about bringing Dunhill to life again.

To Callum's gratitude, Dar had offered to come in a months' time. Mayhap a wee bit later depending on the complexity of some family undertakings. It would be nice to have his friend and brethren in residence.

He had much to accomplish and would see Maggie flourish the way she deserved. Not that she hadn't been happy at Dunhill. He believed she had. But knowing how much she loved Seagrave, he decided it was time to bring Dunhill back to its glory.

Callum felt the weight of so much at the moment. Maggie and her happiness *here*, with him, in what amounted to another lifetime.

Restoring the legacy his father left for him. God's bones, what must the mighty Fergus Donnan O'Roarke think of his son now?

And, lastly, and perhaps most importantly, he'd honor the bargain his mother sought on his behalf.

CHAPTER TWENTY-NINE

By Maggie's count, she lasted forty-six days, twelve hours, and nine minutes. Forty-two of those endured back at Dunhill.

She'd done her best to keep the wall erected around her heart, to self persevere, while still being supportive of her husband. Callum was a good man. Each day, it became more difficult to tell herself she didn't love him, like *that*.

Self-preservation still won out. For now. As long as she was uncertain about how long she'd be in the fifteenth century, she'd continue to resist.

On the other side of this, was the vow she made to support and honor him in all he did. She was his wife, after all, no matter how much magic or forces of fate brought her to his doorstep.

It was startling, still, to think about—she'd literally shown up at his door and become the other half of his life. The second half of his life.

She had no complaints. Life was fine, good even. Actually, who was she kidding? It was amazing. Most of the time she felt she was walking on air. That's how happy she was.

When she'd told as much to Callum, he'd laughed and said this was how she'd appeared to him almost from the first. A woman who floated through the castle instead of merely walking. He said he'd enjoyed watching her glide through the halls and down the stairs, from a distance shortly after she'd arrived, and then from up close.

As soon as they returned to the keep from Seagrave, despite the cold chill of winter creeping in, Callum began opening Dunhill. He did so with an enthusiasm she hadn't known he possessed. To be frank, she'd never seen him so occupied on the grounds before. From sunrise to sunset and some days longer.

Of course, this time of the year, the days were short. But still, he worked tirelessly.

Week by week, Maggie noticed more and more people inhabiting their land. Vacant cottages were now becoming occupied. Their numbers were growing. At this rate Dunhill might be at full steam by spring.

When harsh weather or darkness forced him inside, Callum spoke to her about bringing the castle back to its former glory. Maggie wasn't sure what was driving him so, but she couldn't help getting swept up in his zeal.

As far as she was concerned, the inside of the estate had always been lovely. Though, on further reflection she noted its style *was* only Callum's. She liked the idea of making it, this, their home together.

They'd begun upstairs merely by opening up all the doors. Together, they walked through each chamber, taking a mental inventory. Then began rearranging the furniture, the tapestries and rushes, true pieces d'art, and the bric-a-brac.

The turret chamber that was Callum's, the one he'd shared briefly with Fiona, became theirs over the course of a few weeks. Maggie delighted in bringing in fresh evergreen boughs and dried lavender to decorate, while Nessa and Rose worked on new linens and a coverlet for their bed.

The apartment that had been his parents was slowly becoming a lovely guest suite, and not the shrine it once was. Whatever clothing and shoes Maggie was able to use, they'd moved to their own closets and the dressing area at the other end of the hallway. The rest, for now, they'd packed up together in beautifully crafted chests Callum made himself.

He told her Rose's husband could reupholster any of the furnishings and so she began picking new fabrics from the sewing room, trying out various color and pattern schemes over the course of an afternoon.

The change in Callum filled her with pride, and she wondered if it was her coming here, their relationship and marriage that had made the difference. She had to admit, when she wasn't worried about the what ifs, she felt it too.

The optimism and excitement of a fresh start.

It was enough to make one get up in the morning with renewed vigor and see the world differently. Making this place a home, seeing Callum eager to do the same alongside her, caused Maggie to feel more secure than she had in years.

Callum made love to her early every morning. Often before the sun rose, so eager to start his days. She enjoyed it, of course, the closeness of him, and was an ardent and willing participant. Maggie held herself back from giving herself over to him completely. If she was to continue being happy here, for however long, she felt strongly she couldn't let her guard down.

Not again.

Each night he held out his hand to walk with her upstairs and make love to her before they went to sleep. She'd never been much of a cuddler, and was always surprised since that first night they 'd slept together, really slept together, that whenever she awoke she was stuck to him like glue.

She apologized at first, but on the second or third night they'd been back, Callum told her, "I like holding you. I like you nestled up as close as can be. Mayhap we need this now, having been deprived of the touch of another soul for such a longtime. Mayhap we've become anchors for one another."

The man had a point. Gwen was right, these men were wise beyond their years, and the years they were born in.

In between all this business, Callum still made time to continue her sword lessons. Twice a week he came to find her in the Great Room, solarium, or parlor where she might be redecorating, or stealing away to finish reading a story she'd plucked from one of the shelves. She'd found many of Isabeau's favorites, and they were becoming hers too. She'd usually be so wrapped up in whatever it was she was doing, he'd stopped asking her to join him for lessons, and would just call, "Fetch your sword, Margaret," from the front door.

There was something she found so endearing, so special really, when he used her proper name. Aside from introductions, no one ever really called her Margaret, not even her mother. She'd always been just plain Maggie.

She remembered how Callum used it the night of their wedding, and how it had affected her. When he'd been as frenzied as she, it caused her to come undone. It also had a note of respect, of authority—she was his *wife*. She had importance. So, when he used it now, *it* had importance.

He made her feel that way and showed her daily.

One night after supper, she'd fallen asleep while they lay upon a settee in the Great Room. When she'd awoken alone, she'd gone in search of him and found him in his study. He was whittling by candlelight.

Intrigued, she watched as he set down whatever it was to rotate his wrist this way and that, flexing his fingers for a time. He was obviously taking great pains at what he was doing. When he saw her, he smiled an easy smile and waved her inside. She'd never seen him actually working on something, and was excited to see this new creation.

When she asked him what he was making, he'd held out his hand and pulled her around his desk, settling her on his lap. Then he'd picked up the small object, laying it in the palm of his hand.

Her eyes teared up as she looked at the replica of a jax, so painstakingly carved. She couldn't imagine the time he'd spent making this. Or for that matter, where or when he'd *found* the time. Her gaze grew soft, and she rasped out, "Callum." A tear escaped her eye, and she shook her head.

"You made this? For *me*?" Her voice caught. He smiled softly, wiping her errant tears. He then reached for the pouch hanging from the knob on the tabletop of his desk.

"Hold out your hands," he'd said, looking into her eyes. He brushed the hair back from her face and over her shoulder. Then he'd shook out the contents into her cupped hands... a set of jax fell. She'd counted ten perfectly carved jax when he added the one he'd been holding to the pile. "I just finished the last."

She looked at the beautiful, intricate pieces. Each spike finished with a tiny, rounded ball on the end. Maggie was overcome with gratitude and the feeling of really being known. So overwhelmed with something she couldn't quite put her finger on, she cried. Much to his confusion, she'd ugly cried, too, just for a minute. He held her, patting her back while shushing and there-there-ing her.

"Margaret, what's *this*?"

She smiled through her tears and she could tell from the slight shake of his shoulders and his wink, he'd used *this* again on purpose. It had taken her a moment to find her voice. "*This* is the nicest, most thoughtful gift I've ever received, Callum. Thank you."

"I wished to bring you joy, not tears."

"You've brought more joy to my life than I ever imagined possible." She'd smiled then, meaning it. "And here, so far in the past."

He'd held the pouch open so she could drop the jax back inside. Afterward, he walked her upstairs to bed, where he made love to her and whispered words of endearment in her ear.

So yes, all was going swimmingly—*until it wasn't.*

Then everything turned on a dime. Her spiral into the abyss started that morning when she'd suddenly had that pukey feeling you get when you feel like the back of your throat is dizzy, and your mouth starts to water. Callum left to work outside, so at least she didn't have a witness while she dry-heaved.

Maggie had just run through everything she'd eaten the night before when she realized with a start she was late for her period. Something that never happened in her entire life. Like the sun rose and set, even in different centuries, but Maggie was always on time.

She was so stunned, for a moment she forgot how nauseated she felt. She and Derek never had one pregnancy scare in all their years together, and they hadn't *always* been careful. In the back of her mind, Maggie worried maybe this meant she couldn't have children. Or maybe they'd need a bit of fertility help when the time came.

An intense wave of nausea brought her back to the present, and she clutched her stomach, thinking of the life she and Callum may have created together.

She was going to have his baby.

Her head fell back as tears of joy and laughter bubbled forth because she knew quite forcefully this was what she wanted. Maggie was so overwhelmed by this rush of joy, it stunned her. Something else became immediately clear to her, too. She loved—L-O-V-E-D—loved this man, and she couldn't deny how much.

The walls crumbled and if he looked at her now, he'd clearly see through. He deserved her love and she would tell him tonight. Regardless of what might happen, she could no longer live in the fear of *what if.*

Later that afternoon, while she was helping Nessa and Rose arrange some of Isabeau's treasured knickknacks in the Great Hall, Maggie heard what sounded like a stampede rise from the courtyard. The smile she'd been fighting to keep off her face vanished in an instant. Knowing what that signified the last time, she was on immediate, high alert.

She ran to see what was happening, and stopped on the front steps to find Callum in all his glory—her proud warrior—surrounded by his comrades as they made way for the keep's doors. Her breath still caught when she saw him at times, and she couldn't believe by some odd twist of fate, he was her chosen one. She even forgot to add *in this century* this time.

Maggie stood, frozen in the archway of the Great Hall. When Callum saw her there he locked his eyes on hers, with a serious, determined look. In the months she'd known him, she'd come to know all sides of him. The gentle soul she first met and now this implacable warrior.

She loved each and every part of him. Every single inch inside and out. How had she ever doubted that?

The depth of her admission was astonishing, and all but knocked her to the ground. She physically wavered from it. Then he was there, holding her steady.

Maggie clutched his shoulders. "Where are you going?"

"There's trouble to the South."

"Wait." She ran to their room and grabbed the sword, breathless when she returned.

"I haven't seen this in years." Dar said in surprise, for he and Graham had joined Callum on the steps. His eyes narrowed, and a puzzled look crossed his face, just like everyone else's when they noticed the hilt now held the stone.

Then, unexpectedly, Dar reached out and grasped the hilt, taking the sword in his hand. He held it aloft and then his eyes went wide, and Maggie's too, as the sword buzzed, and the jewel glowed.

G-L-O-W-E-D.

Maggie felt the reverberation from two feet away. The same she'd felt the day she'd been transported here so long ago. So long ago she'd stopped counting the days since she'd left the twenty-first century, and instead only counted the days since she'd been married to Callum.

Reflexively, her hand shot out toward the sword, images of home, Celeste, and the life she'd left behind flashing across her vision. Then, just as suddenly, she jumped back, scrambling as far away as she could, terrified at what she'd almost done, hoping it wasn't too late.

Please God, don't make me go back. Not now. She kept chanting her prayer, her eyes squeezed shut.

At the clatter of the sword landing on the ground, she opened them to see Dar shaking his arm, clearly uncertain exactly what was at play, but smart enough to let it go. Both men stared at her a moment. Then something crossed Callum's face, and he bent down to retrieve the now unanimated sword and normal looking stone.

❧ CHAPTER THIRTY ❧

Callum went to his wife, who retreated to a cower behind the stone column.

"Maggie," he said. His own thoughts racing at what he had just witnessed. *Could it be true?* Her actions had certainly been very telling. The fear plain as day on her face. Seeing her in such distress, he pushed his own thoughts aside and held out his hand, "Come, love."

Her eyes darted from the stone to Dar and then to him.

"It's stopped. See." He turned it over in his hand to show her, yet she scrambled back. He tried to hand the sword off to Dar, but Dar shook his head as if he'd held the plague in his grasp and threw his hands up in the air.

Sighing, Callum set the sword down and approached his wife. "Margaret. Please."

"Callum," Dar warned. "We must go."

He knew this, as the grumbles of the men grew louder. But he was torn leaving her so. Callum shook his head, standing in front of her as she looked up at him. "I'll—"

"Be safe," she breathed. "Please, Callum."

He matched her stare, her eyes taking in every part of his face. It was the same look she'd worn when they were at the lake and she thought she would drown. Before he could say anything, she turned and ran back into the keep, and up the stairs.

It was as he walked to the stables, the weight of the sword in his hand, that the whirling in his head cleared enough to make sense of what he believed just occurred. He mounted his horse, still turning the thought over in his mind.

His wife had chosen him.

She was given a chance. He'd seen it plain as day, the sword illuminating for the first time since she'd arrived at the Abbey.

She chose him.

For a moment, he'd known true fear when the sword shook in Dar's hand. The split-second Maggie's hand reached in its direction almost killed him. Then she'd jumped back as if burned, her own matching terror plain on her face.

Callum knew then without even a shred of doubt, she loved him. She loved the life they had and were in fact making together. God's bones everything he did was for her. Her happiness was paramount to all, but he was done placating her fear.

He would settle this for once and for all.

Wheeling his horse around, Callum made for the bailey instead of the gates.

His footfall must have announced his presence because she opened their chamber door just as he reached it, stepping back when she saw his determined look and the set of his jaw.

"Tell me, Margaret." He said moving forward as she continued to retreat.

"Tell you what, Callum?" She whispered, not quite looking him in the eye.

"What you've purposely *not* said despite your feelings. What you've asked me not to say either. Enough of this. Do you hear me, I say enough!"

"Please don't."

"I have been precisely as scared as you." God's Bones, his heart felt like it lay in a vice at times he loved her so much. 'Twas the last thing he wanted. Ever. To feel this way, again. And yet, here it was, but deeper for their experience and loss. From the very first, he felt like Maggie belonged to him. Not by creed, or right, chauvinistic as it might sound. But by God, fate, destiny, take the pick. Maggie belonged to him on a level soul deep. He felt it and knew she did too. "But only because we keep dancing around what is so. 'Tis ours to take and God's bones, I say we take it."

She shook her head, her soft, wavy curls swaying this way and that. He moved to stand before her, gently lifting her chin as the back of his fingers swept up the column of her neck.

"Say it," he said, an order, but softly.

"Please, Callum."

He waited until she met his gaze. "I love you, Margaret Siobhan Sinclair O'Roarke."

As a feeling of freedom swept through him at the words, she gasped and stepped back.

"Don't say that out loud," she cried in a whisper. "Did you see what just happened! It's all my fault!"

"What's your fault?"

"I thought it. I thought it and now it wants me back! We *are* cursed," she said emphatically, nodding her head.

"Nae!" In either case. For one, he did not think *it* wanted her back. Not that he would ever let her go. In truth and for fact, the sword did not glow for Maggie.

It did so for Dar.

As to the other, he'd tread old territory once more. "We are *not* cursed, Maggie. We are *not* responsible for the death of Fiona, nor for Derek. We are not reliving a nightmare to recur again and again. Fate would never be so cruel. I swear it to be so." He repeated this twice more, knowing it was a fear of hers. He was determined to find this enchantress come spring and put this to rest.

She glanced a look at him, and his heart broke at what he was afraid she would say.

"But what if we *are*, Callum? I had the most incredible feeling of joy earlier. I thought those things about you and me, and look what happened. It glowed! What if we have to keep reliving again and again feeling this way, only to lose it in the end. What if—"

"Enough." Callum shook his head, and took a step forward, gathering her in his arms. She stiffened a moment before relaxing into his embrace. He loved holding this woman. Her frame fit perfectly tucked against him. Then she burrowed into him and rubbed her cheek on his chest. "Look at me, Maggie."

She pulled back, her eyes wide and trusting.

"I know you are scared," he said. "There's a reason we are together, Margaret Siobhan. I'm not sure how or why, simply that it is so." He cupped her face in his hands and then kissed her. "Tell me," he said.

She looked as if she might speak, but nothing came out.

"Tell me," he said again.

"I... I... I'm pregnant."

The statement stunned him. Like a blow, he stumbled back, then steeled his expression. Margaret was barren. He'd been sure of it. She'd spent ten childbearing years with Derek. While the realization had been devastating at the time, he'd given it much thought and was at peace not being able to have children. In fact, he'd come to believe it was for the best.

He and Margaret and their love were enough.

Callum turned to look out the window as unbidden thoughts crowded his mind of the last time he'd heard words such as those. And the horrors that had followed. When he turned back to Maggie, he didn't know what to say. Didn't know how to voice all he was feeling, the good and the bad.

So, he did the only thing he could think of.

"I must go." He told her, then he turned and left.

❦CHAPTER THIRTY-ONE❧

The doors of Seagrave swung open, silently accepting Maggie's arrival, as she climbed the front stairs. Gwen padded through the foyer, baby in hand, and turned to see who was coming or going. She startled at seeing her.

"Maggie? What are you doing here?" She asked, meeting her just inside the threshold.

Maggie grasped Gwen's free hand. "I... I... I just need somewhere I can think. Somewhere, I know..."

But she didn't know.

She'd run away.

Maggie had stood in the center of the chamber she shared with Callum, heartbroken. She'd meant to tell him she loved him and instead blurted out she was pregnant. The look he gave her, the silence that followed, and his deliberate turn as she watched him walk away shattered her.

She'd been so stunned, she couldn't move until she heard him ride off with his men minutes later. Shaking, she'd wiped her tears, and not sure of what to do, grabbed her satchel. She'd packed a few days' clothing and her treasures, the set of jax she'd brought with her, her phone, and nestled amongst her dresses and underthings, the new set Callum made for her.

As she walked to the threshold of their room, she reached for Callum's sword, the replacement. God forbid she had to defend herself.

She'd left a note for Nessa and Rose, knowing they'd show Albert immediately. But really, what could they do? It's not like he could text Callum and tell him she'd left.

Edward was already done with his stable duties for the night. With everyone riding off only a short time ago, she was able to take her mare with no one the wiser. She'd taken the pass that would lead her to the lodge, grateful she was able to remember it. There, she and her horse rested a bit. With a full moon to guide her, she'd set off. And after a few hours made Seagrave just as the sun was rising.

She was still geeked up on adrenalin, but just beneath the surface exhaustion nipped and bayed.

"Wait." Gwen paused then, and looked over Maggie's shoulder and out into the bailey. "Where's Callum?" She asked. Gwen's eyes went wide then, and she squeezed her hand, in that franticness just before your suspicions are confirmed. "He doesn't know you're here, does he?" Gwen all but yelled in her face.

At this, her eyes darted toward the men who stood by the doors. *Yeah, like they didn't hear.*

Maggie just shook her head. "Callum left with Dar and his men. They were going off... They went off with their swords."

"Oh, dear." Gwen looked down then and seemed to consider something a fraction of a second before shouting, "Husband!"

Maggie squeezed her hand back. "Gwen, what are you doing?"

"He's going to find out. We have to tell him now." She shook her head. "I told you, band-aid quick. It's the only way."

Greylen made his way down the stairs, toddler in hand. They were obviously all on their way to the kitchen for breakfast. He gave Maggie a confused smile, then asked his wife why she'd called for him.

"Maggie came to stay with us," was all Gwen said, and Maggie gave a silent thanks.

Greylen shook his head, rolled his eyes and said to Gwen, "Aye, wife, I can see that." The sarcasm was slight, but right now she envied the affection and love these two shared.

Gwen sighed. "Greylen, Maggie came to stay with us."

Greylen rolled his eyes when she repeated herself. "You'll have to forgive my wife, Maggie. She's prone to fits of daftness."

He looked at Gwen affectionately, then a moment later, his head snapped in her direction and suddenly he was the fifteenth century laird and warrior she knew him to be.

"Callum doesn't know you're here? You came alone?" He looked out into the courtyard this way and that. "You rode here without his or anyone's knowledge?" His voice grew louder with each word until Gwen put a hand on his arm in an attempt to calm him. Their children didn't flinch, obviously used to the raucousness. "Do you know how he lost his wife?" Greylen said, turning to her. "Have you any idea what he might think when he returns and you're not there, but instead had run off?" He made it worse and shouted. "Alone!"

Maggie's heart sank, realizing she'd just recreated Callum's worst fear. Her face fell, and she started to cry. In between gasps, she choked out. "I... I told him I was pregnant."

She sank to her knees as Greylen roared, and stayed on the cold stone floor while Gwen tried to calm her.

CHAPTER THIRTY-TWO

Maggie languished at Seagrave for five long nights and six even longer days. She could barely eat, not only from morning sickness, but because she was heartsick. She didn't know it was a real thing. Being heartsick.

It was.

It was more debilitating than anything she'd been through these last years. And that said it all. All she wanted was a redo of that day back at Dunhill. A chance to tell Callum if she was given the choice between going back to her life in the future, or building a future *here*, now with him, there *was* no choice.

She'd pick him.

Hands down every single time.

She'd raise every white flag necessary in surrender. Even more, she'd fight for them. She loved him. She was in love with him. And she would do anything, *give* anything for the chance to make things right.

She could see now it had been shock he'd felt when she told him she was pregnant. What with Dar urging him to get going on an admittedly important life or death journey and the surprise of her declaration, Maggie understood his reaction.

According to Greylen, Callum had been under the impression she couldn't have children. She could understand why he would think that, and honestly, she was surprised he'd considered it at all. But that was Callum, moving full steam ahead with plans for their lives together, while she'd teetered on the edge, terrified of crossing the line.

She felt small and selfish now that she kept a piece of herself from Callum. The man who'd given her everything in his power to give, and she couldn't tell him how much she loved him and adored him.

It was different being at Seagrave this time. Only weeks ago, Maggie couldn't wait to come back.

Now all she wanted was to go home.

But Greylen refused to let her leave, even with an escort. He told her he'd sent word to Callum, she was here and safe, and would remain under their care until he could collect her. He'd said in their custody just to make a point. At first Greylen had been, understandably, angry on his friend's behalf. It was a small blessing he'd come around shortly after.

Isabelle and Gavin, who she had been looking forward to meeting, albeit under different circumstances, were in residence for a few weeks, too. They'd been atop the landing when she'd first arrived and had watched the whole scene play out below. Suffice it say, Maggie hadn't made the best first impression. Still, it turned out they were pretty great. Though no real surprise knowing Gwen and Greylen.

Maggie was on the receiving end of lots of compassionate looks and *there-theres* from the men, while Gwen and Isabelle did their best to cheer her up. She shared her jax with the girls. Not the set Callum made for her; those she'd only displayed for their view. So proud to show them off, bragging of his talent. She'd even added, while extending her hand, he'd crafted her wedding band himself. They didn't mind hearing it the first two days, but after that, they rolled their eyes at her, tired of her extolling his virtues.

She tried, she really did. But all she wanted was to see Callum. Assure him she was okay. Tell him she loved him. And beg him. B-E-G beg him to forgive her. She hoped they could get back—find a new better than where they used to be.

Late one afternoon she was standing before the window in her chamber, when suddenly the silhouette of a rider appeared far off on the horizon. Chills consumed her at the sight of who she hoped was her husband, the father of her child. Face and hands pressed to the glass, she held her breath until she made out his colors dancing in the wind from the back of his saddle. Tears streaming down her face, Maggie watched him race across the path leading to the crest just beyond the walls of Seagrave.

The gates opened as he approached, and she ran.

As she rounded the landing, the doors swung open. Callum bellowed her name.

"*Margaret Siobhan O'Roarke!*" Then there was a pause. "*Show yourself!*"

She ran across the foyer and through the doors, stopping short on the portico. Callum stood there, sword drawn, as if he intended to do battle. It was then Maggie really saw the state of him.

She froze, and her hands flew to her mouth.

The left side of his face was caked in dried blood. It covered his clothes on the same side, too. He rubbed his free arm across his forehead when she appeared, focused on her, then wavered and collapsed. Falling to the ground so hard, plumes of dirt rose around him.

Maggie screamed, a bloodcurdling scream from the top of her lungs. Then she ran, collapsing beside him, sobbing his name.

"Nae! Callum! Nae nae nae!"

The rest happened in a blur out of some god-awful horror movie. Someone dragged her off of his body and held her back as Greylen turned Callum over, shouting his name. Gwen was there next, kneeling beside him, checking his vitals. She started shaking her head, and at this, Maggie assumed the worst and started screaming all over again.

Her worst nightmare come to life.

All over again.

For the second time in two centuries, she had to live with loss.

They *were* cursed.

Guilt consumed her. Why had she kept her feelings from him? It seemed pointless now, he'd never known how much he meant to her. How very much she loved him. That they were having a baby. She was crying so hard she started gasping and choking.

"Put her down, Kevin." Gwen shouted to their man in arms.

Like a dog, on her hands and knees, Maggie cried and coughed so hard she threw up, then curled into a ball.

She stared blankly at Callum's body, watching as men ran toward him carrying an old wooden door. She continued to stare as Greylen and Gavin turned him on his side so they could shimmy the mock stretcher beneath him, and roll him onto it.

It took six men to hoist his weight. She pawed the dirt in front of her in a futile attempt to reach out to him, as they took him away and carried him toward the keep. Maggie mustered enough strength to swat the hands away that tried to move her.

She wanted to stay there and die.

Against her last wishes, someone scooped her up. The comforting and lulling "Shh" to her surprise came from Greylen.

"He's okay, Maggie," he said, his voice calm. "Just exhausted, not truly hurt. It appears in his hurry, he never stopped or took any rest. All he needs is some sleep and water. Gwen says, he'll be right as rain, whatever that means."

A poor cat howled in pain somewhere. It was a God awful sound and Maggie just wanted it to stop. Then, as Greylen held her closer and rocked her, she realized the noise, quieted now in her comfort, had come from her.

Still disoriented and confused, she was carried behind Callum to a room close to the kitchen Maggie had never seen before. One she could only describe as an infirmary. It wasn't state-of-the art by any means. But it looked like Gwen could provide a modicum of help when needed.

Greylen set her on a chair next to a slated table they transferred Callum to. Then Gwen called for hot water as she looked at Maggie. "Help me get him washed up, then they can move him upstairs."

They bathed him by hand, and Maggie combed the dirt from his hair before washing and rinsing it. Greylen came back with a soft pair of drawstring britches they got him into. Then they took him upstairs on the now cleaned door draped with a fresh sheet, obviously used to transfer patients.

Gwen assured her, he was fine. She couldn't say when he'd been injured, but explained to Maggie head wounds bleed a lot, making them look worse than they might be. She'd left a jar of ointment on the nightstand so Maggie could reapply it when necessary.

Now, Maggie stood next to him, tucking the covers around him and brushing her fingers through his hair, while Anna saw to a hot bath in her room.

She was a mess.

When Maggie had finally assured herself Callum would be okay, that she didn't need to stand sentry all evening, she crawled into bed beside him.

At first, she worried about disturbing him, but he reflexively gathered her close.

It was the last thing she remembered after whispering, "I love you."

CHAPTER THIRTY-THREE

Callum awoke slowly. His eyes heavy, and his body spent. The sweet redolence of Maggie's scent and her body tucked up tight against him was a vital balm to his soul. He breathed in deep, his eyelids still too heavy to open. Then to his chagrin his shoulders trembled from within and gave to silent, wracking sobs as his arms tightened around her.

He felt her tears on his chest as she wept with him. God's bones. 'Twas the worst week of his life. Even word of her safety did little to ease his mind.

He'd in essence shunned his expectant wife. His fair Margaret, who's only obstacle was beyond her control. Her sorrow of leaving Celeste, and fear of loving and losing again, living in the uncertainty of her permanence here, with him.

In his estimation, neither a true slight.

Margaret had become the reason he awoke early every morn filled with the thirst to live life again to the fullest. Fate, fortune, and God had afforded them this chance again, this opportunity at love and life brimming with fulfillment.

From this day forward, it would not be in vain.

He opened his eyes, slowly lifting his wife to the pillow. Her hand gently brushed his face, then came to rest at the nape of his neck. He shook his head as he looked at her, "Margaret." 'Twas a rasp, but he managed. "I missed you, love."

'Twas not what he'd intended to say first, but so overcome, 'twas what spilled forth from his mouth. His lips whisked across her forehead and eyes. "I never thought we'd have a babe of our own."

"But?" She said expectantly, her eyes filled with worry.

"Nae, no but." He shook his head again. "We can fill all of Dunhill if that be fate's will."

"I love you, Callum."

"I know you do, Margaret."

"You do?" Relief shone in her eyes.

He smiled. "Aye, you show me every day, love. In everything you do. I love you more than life itself, Margaret of O'Roarke. You are the sun that feeds my soul. In truth, my everything."

"I love you, too, Callum of O'Roarke. You make me happier than I ever thought possible."

"Even here?"

"Aye, even here."

"Then I say, it's time we live, love, and truly be merry."

"Let it be so." She whispered.

His hand skimmed the side of her face, and he kissed her. "Aye, my love. Let it be so."

❧EPILOGUE❧

Maggie and Callum walked hand in hand through the spring fair, wending their way around tents where the families camped overnight and toward the booths set up for those selling their wares. They'd stopped twice already to partake in a few bites of delicious food, but Maggie was already thinking about what they would try next. Her stomach was round and taut with their baby growing inside.

It seemed that lately she had a growing affection for almost everything.

Dar, who had been staying at Dunhill for the past several weeks, called out to them to wait. It was the third time something caught his eye and Maggie chuckled, tugging Callum's hand and pointed back toward his friend. Her husband took the opportunity to pull her in close for a kiss while Dar caught up with them.

He joined them with a broad smile on his face, which Maggie returned. She'd become fond of Dar since he'd come to stay with them. She liked having him around. In fact, he'd taken over the guest suite that had been Callum's parents'.

He was funny but intense, and truly good-hearted. I mean, the guy stayed at Dunhill to help Callum after he'd run himself into the ground. Literally. Maggie suspected Dar leaned toward Callum, as Callum did toward Grey.

His obsession with hearing stories about the twenty-first century made him remind her of that guy from the first Terminator movie. In reverse of course, since Dar lived in the past but was fascinated by the future.

Just a week or so ago, she'd opened up to him about how she'd arrived in the fifteenth century. She didn't know Callum had told *all* his brethren about her and her origin. It made sense, she guessed, seeing as they all knew about Gwen. Once she ascertained Dar wouldn't be freaked out, quite the opposite turned out to be true—he was captivated with the future and was full of questions for her. So, Maggie told him stories and showed him what she could on her phone. She'd finally managed to get the solar battery to recharge.

When she broke down one night over how desperately she missed Celeste and her worry she would think Maggie abandoned her, Dar offered to carry a message to her. Maggie had a feeling he was more taken with Celeste, than with the thought of the future itself, but still. He often stared at her photo for quite some time. It was sweet.

Dar reached for the sword again to see if it would glow. It did. For the time being, they all decided it would be best if they kept a hands-off policy where Dar was concerned. The last thing they wanted was for him to go time-traveling to God knows where until he was really and truly ready.

Just as Dar reached them, Maggie's attention was caught by something else. She, gasped and gripped Callum's hand tightly. Her eyes on a woman with beautiful red hair and eyes so vibrantly green, they appeared to glow.

She was young—much, much younger than when Maggie had first met her, but there was no denying fact. The woman inclined her head and smiled, coming to a stop before them. She looked from Maggie to Callum and back again, then down at her belly. She covered it with her hand. "I see you've found each other. Another boy to carry the family name. Your father Fergus would be mighty proud." She said, smiling warmly at Callum as Maggie just stood there, stunned. "To answer your question, you are each other's true loves. You had already found each other, but fate sometimes, she is fickle. You were granted another chance with the bargain your mother made, Callum."

Then, as if things weren't weird enough, she pointed to Dar. "Prepare him well. The future may not be ready for him, but he indeed will be ready for it. Celeste waits. The time is almost near."

With that, she left. Maggie craned her neck to see where she had gone. But it was as if she'd disappeared into thin air. Maybe she had.

Her husband turned to her, smiling at her with all the love he showered her with each and every day. "My queen, are you now satisfied?"

She inclined her head demurely and curtsied as if he were king. "My Liege Lord, I am now and forever at your service."

ACKNOWLEDGMENTS

I am so thankful for my talented, amazing team at Taggart Press. They are the reasons why my books are beautiful on the inside and out, and work tirelessly to get my books discovered by readers.

Sarah Beaudin
Interior design and production · C'est Beau Designs

Brittany Elges
Copy-editing and proofreading · Writers Wingman

Marian Hussey
Audiobook Narrator / Voice Talent

George Long
Cover design · G-Force Design

Bonnie Paulson
Business and advertising consulting · Finding Your Indie

Katie Price
Website development and design · Priceless Design Studio

Liz Psaltis
Content creation, advertising, and promotion · EHP Marketing

Mandie Stevens
Social media management, promotion, advertising management, and conferences · Finding Your Indie

Rachel Stout
Developmental editing · Rachel Stout Editorial Services

Jane Ubell-Meyer
Luxury hotel amenity placement, major media coverage, and events · Bedside Reading

Made in the USA
Middletown, DE
09 July 2021

43742895R00168